The word was barely ⬛⬛⬛⬛⬛
closer, bending his he⬛ ⬛⬛⬛ ⬛⬛⬛⬛

"What?"

"I said yes. I'll marry you."

"Thank you."

"I think it should be the other way around. I should be thanking you," Brittany said tiredly, finally giving in to the urge to lean her face against his hand. There was such strength in him. And she needed that strength right now. "I feel as if I'm using you. If it wasn't for the baby…"

"If it wasn't for the baby, the situation would be completely different," he agreed. "But that isn't the case. There's nothing wrong with taking help from a friend."

She laughed, barely holding back the sob that threatened to escape. "I think this is going a little above and beyond the call of friendship, but I can't argue anymore."

*Also available from MIRA Books and*
*DALLAS SCHULZE*

**HOME TO EDEN**

# The
# Vow
# Dallas
# Schulze

**MIRA BOOKS**

**MIRA**

ISBN 1-55166-295-7

THE VOW

Copyright © 1990 by Dallas Schulze.

MIRA and the star colophon are trademarks of MIRA Books.

**Printed in U.S.A.**

# The Vow

# Chapter One

"We are gathered here today to say farewell to two people, a father and his son, who meant a great deal to all of us. Larry Remington was a respected member of our small community. His passing will leave a gap in many lives. And Dan Remington, a true son of Remembrance, was born into our town, spending all of his tragically short life among us."

Michael tuned out the pastor's voice. He didn't need someone else to tell him how great his loss was. Dan had been his best friend. His absence was like a knotted fist in the pit of his stomach. It just didn't seem possible. Plane crash in Central America or no, Dan simply couldn't be dead.

But he was. No survivors. Dan, his father, the whole archaeology team gone in an instant. The pilot had managed to radio their coordinates as the plane was going down. They had served only as a guide to the burned-out wreckage.

Michael stared at the back of the seat in front of him. The pastor was droning on about Dan's life, his career aspirations. Why the hell did they always have to talk about what could have been at these things? Was it supposed to make it easier for everyone to hear a litany of everything that would never happen?

He glanced across the aisle and felt the knot in his stomach tighten. Brittany. What was she thinking? Feeling? As he watched, she reached up, her fingers grasping the gold heart pendant that was her only jewelry. Dan had given her that last Christmas. Michael remembered him picking it out, laughing that it was certainly more decorative than wearing his heart on his sleeve.

His eyes traced the delicate lines of her profile. She looked so fragile, so helpless. Her thick black hair was drawn back in a simple knot, baring the slender length of her neck. Her skin was so pale it seemed translucent. He wanted to go to her, put his arm around her and tell her that everything was going to be all right. The intensity of his desire to soothe her pain made him uneasy, and he looked away.

Dan had been his best friend. Brittany was the woman he'd loved. It was an extension of Michael's friendship that made him want to comfort Brittany. Besides, he liked Brittany for her own sake. Had liked her since the moment Dan had introduced them. In fact, if Dan hadn't— He shrugged the thought away. Brittany had clearly thought the sun rose and set on Dan Remington. Her pain must run deep.

His eyes were drawn to her again. She really was lovely. She seemed to feel his gaze, for her eyes lifted, meeting his. They were almost the same gray as her dress. Michael had never thought of gray as a warm color until he'd met Brittany and seen how full of life and fire her eyes were. Now the fire was quenched, the life dulled, her pain obvious. He gave her a crooked smile. The corners of her mouth lifted in acknowledgment before her eyes dropped back to her hands.

Michael was more or less successful in blocking out the majority of the service. When it ended at last, he stood, hunching his shoulders against the ache that had settled in the middle of his back. The other mourners were filing into the vestibule at the front of the church. There would be food set out, sustenance for those left behind.

The last thing Michael wanted to do was nibble stuffed mushrooms and make small talk about what a terrible tragedy this had been. His grief was a private thing, not something he wanted to share over tea and crumpets. He turned, planning to make his exit out another door. Catching a glimpse of pale gray, he hesitated. Brittany's full skirt disappeared into the vestibule.

There was nothing he could say to her, no comfort he could offer, which didn't explain why he changed his plans and followed her into the other room.

Everything was just as he'd expected. People stood around in small groups, talking quietly, sipping coffee and fruit juice from paper cups and shaking their heads over the tragic waste of it all.

*"If only Larry hadn't been so determined to go on this foolish trip…. Well, yes, it had been a dream of his for years, but he'd certainly been well past the age of going on wild-goose chases. And to take Dan with him…. True, Dan had been as excited by the idea of an archaeological expedition as his father. But look where it had gotten the pair of them. And there was poor Clare, left alone. And at her age."*

Michael made his way through the gathering, careful to meet no one's eye, his face set in an expression that did not invite approach. His blue eyes skimmed the group.

"Michael Sinclair. I didn't realize you were here."

He stiffened and then turned reluctantly. Merideth Wallings was quite possibly the worst gossip the world had ever known. She was also shallow, grasping and generally unpleasant. Unfortunately, her family owned half of Remembrance, and she'd grown accustomed to the deference this tended to purchase for her.

"Mrs. Wallings." He nodded, trying to look as if he had other places to go. Merideth didn't notice.

"Isn't this just the most awful tragedy?" She took a bite of a cracker, her dark eyes snapping with excitement. "It's just impossible to believe that they're dead. Poor Larry. And poor Dan, in the prime of life. You and Dan were quite close, weren't you?"

"We were good friends," Michael said repressively.

"It's just terrible. I don't know how poor Clare is going to manage."

"It will be difficult. If you'll—"

"I don't see your parents here today." Merideth craned her neck as if expecting to see Donovan and Beth lurking in a corner.

"They're on a cruise. I called them with the news, but they couldn't make it back in time for the services."

"That's right. Poor Beth. How is she doing?"

"She's doing just fine."

"It must have been so hard for her to lose the baby."

"These things happen."

"Yes, but it's harder when you get to her age." Merideth crunched a carrot stick.

"She's fine." Michael's eyes grew frosty. A lesser person might have taken notice that she was stepping on shaky ground. Merideth was made of sterner stuff.

"Well, of course, Beth always has been the sort to put up a brave front. You know, at her age, it was risky to try a pregnancy to start with. We can't stay young forever, you know. I could have told her, if only she'd asked me, that it was a mistake to try for a child at this late date. It's just too dangerous. It's a shame Donovan—" She broke off, shaking her head, her mouth turned up in a grimace she appeared to think was an indulgent smile. "But then, men can be so foolish about this sort of thing. They just don't think about the risks we women take."

"Mrs. Wallings, this child was something *both* my parents wanted. Its loss was something they both felt."

"I'm sure it was, Michael. I certainly didn't mean to imply that it wasn't. It's just that these things are always felt more keenly by the woman. After all, we are the ones who carry the child beneath our hearts. I know just how Beth must be feeling right now."

"I seriously doubt that," Michael told her bluntly, annoyance and distraction overtaking him. "Excuse me." He walked away, leaving her with her mouth agape.

He'd spotted Brittany near the window, though even without that excuse, he couldn't have tolerated another minute of Merideth Wallings's sanctimonious claptrap. He moved through the crowd as quickly as politeness allowed, slowing a few paces from Brittany.

Now that he was so close, he suddenly doubted the wisdom of approaching her. After all, they didn't know each other all that well. Dan had been their connecting link, and now that link was gone. She was staring out the window, unaware of him. He could just leave.

But she looked so alone. Her slender figure seemed dragged down by the weight of her simple dress. He had the feeling that the slightest touch might shatter her into a million pieces.

"Brittany." He said her name softly. She started but didn't immediately turn.

"Michael." His name held a wealth of pain, making him wonder if his presence was too great a reminder of her loss. But she reached out, her hand seeking his. Michael took it, feeling the delicacy of her fingers against the callused strength of his palm. He joined her at the window.

Hot summer sunshine blazed down outside, incongruous in the face of the reason they were here. It should have been pouring rain. Brittany must have felt the same thing.

"They shouldn't have funerals in the middle of summer," she said quietly. "Funerals should be for winter, when everything is all cold and grim."

"It does seem wrong, doesn't it?" They stood without speaking for a few moments, their hands still linked.

"It doesn't seem possible," Brittany said, drawing her hand from his to wipe a solitary tear from her cheek.

"No, it doesn't." He wanted to reach out and pull her into his arms, let her cry her grief out on his shoulder. Instead, he pushed his hands into his pockets, reminding himself that it wasn't his place.

"How are you doing?" he asked instead. For the first time, she looked at him.

"I don't really know." Up close, he could see the

smudgy gray shadows beneath her eyes. "And you? Dan always said you two were like brothers. It must be very hard for you."

"Yeah." Michael looked away, gritting his teeth against the ache in his throat. "I'm doing okay."

"No, you're not. Not any more than I am. None of us are." Her voice rose, drawing a few eyes in their direction. She gulped, fighting for control. "It's not fair Michael. It's just not fair."

"I know." He glanced around, noting the attention they were getting. "Come on, let's get out of here." He set his arm around her shoulders, ignoring the questioning looks as he drew her to the door.

Outside, the hot Indiana summer enveloped them, but it couldn't banish the chill of loss. Brittany leaned against him, letting him lead her toward the narrow lawn next to the church.

"Did you bring your car?" he asked.

"No. I got a ride from a friend."

"I'll drive you home."

"Michael." The sudden urgency in her voice brought him to a stop. "I'm going to be sick," she said thinly. One look at her pale face told him that she wasn't kidding and that there was no way she could make it back inside. He steered her around the corner of the church into the relative privacy of a group of bushes.

"Go away," she ordered, the impact lost in the quavering tone of her voice.

"Don't be an idiot." The look she flashed him showed annoyance, but she didn't have a chance to argue. Michael held her head, supporting her trembling body with the strength of his own.

Once the sickness was over, several minutes passed

before she gathered the strength to push him away, standing waveringly on knees that clearly weren't too keen on supporting her.

"You should have left me alone."

He might have showed some penitence if she hadn't had to clutch at his arm when her knees threatened to buckle. He slid an arm around her waist, guiding her shaky footsteps to the scarred water fountain that stood next to the church.

Brittany rinsed her mouth, then she drank thirstily of the cool water. When she was through, Michael dampened his handkerchief and wiped it across her moist forehead. It was a measure of her exhaustion that she didn't protest, closing her eyes and leaning against him as the cool cloth soothed her clammy skin.

"I'm sorry," she murmured.

"Don't be an idiot."

Her eyes came open. "You keep telling me that." Her smile flickered and then broke, her eyes filling with tears. "Maybe I can't help it."

He glanced over his shoulder as the church door opened and several people walked out. "Come on. Let's get out of here."

They didn't speak again until he had his old Mustang on the road, heading away from the church.

"I always liked this car," Brittany said.

Michael barely glanced at the gleaming black paint and immaculate upholstery. He'd spent his last two years in high school working on the junk heap the car had been, restoring it to pristine condition. Right now, he had more important things on his mind.

"How are you feeling?"

"Stupid. Embarrassed."

"There's nothing to be embarrassed about. Are you all right now?"

"Sure." She laughed, a bitter tone in the sound. "I'm just great if you—" She broke off, shaking her head. "I'm fine."

"What were you going to say?"

"Nothing. It's not important." The set of her chin told him he wasn't going to get anything out of her unless she chose to allow it.

He braked for a red light near the center of town, casting a quick look in her direction. She was staring out at the downtown bustle, but he knew she wasn't seeing it. Her gaze was turned inward. There was something wrong—he understood her sense of loss, but her introspection seemed to go beyond Dan's death.

"Brittany." She turned to look at him as the light changed to green. He put the car in gear, half-glad for the excuse not to look at her. Looking at her could easily become a habit. "What's bothering you? There's something more than Dan's—" He stopped, unable to say the word.

"No. No, there's not. At least, nothing that you can help me with. Did I tell you that I'm staying with my parents for a couple of days? You don't have to drive me all the way to Indianapolis."

Michael hesitated. Instinct told him to push her, to make her tell him what was wrong. Good manners dictated that he back off. If she didn't want to tell him, there was no law that said she had to.

"Where do your parents live?"

He followed her directions to a small development on the far edge of town. It was the first tiny square of tract homes to have gone up in Remembrance, back in the fifties. As such, he supposed it had some vague historical significance. But the architect in him winced at the rows of little square houses. The years had given them some individuality, but stripped of the minor changes, they were all identical, all without character.

He pulled up before the house she indicated, a plain white box even more stark than its neighbors. The immaculate lawn looked as if it had been mowed by a surgeon, the trees precisely pruned, the flower beds meticulously edged. The effect should have been lovely. Instead, it was too symmetrical, too perfect.

He turned to Brittany, but she was talking before he could open his mouth. "Thank you for the ride home. I hadn't even thought about how I was going to get back."

"I'll walk you up to the door."

"That's not necessary." But he was already out of the car, coming around to her side to open her door. She took his hand reluctantly, letting him help her out of the car before releasing it.

They walked up the neat brick path in silence. Brittany fumbled in her purse as they stepped onto the narrow porch, Michael's shoes echoing on the wooden floor.

"Got it." She smiled nervously as she pulled out a key and inserted it into the lock. "I'm all the time losing keys. It's a good thing I have a roommate at school who can let me in. Otherwise, I'd probably have to set up camp in the library—"

"Brittany." Michael's quiet voice broke into her babbling. She stopped, sucking in a breath that came near to a sob.

"Michael, please. I can't take much more today."

"I'm not trying to cause you more grief. But I know

there's something wrong. Now that Dan isn't here, I hope you know you can come to me.''

''Oh, Michael.'' Her shoulders slumped for an instant before she straightened them. She looked up at him, her eyes glistening with tears but her chin set. ''There's nothing wrong. I'm just trying to deal with what's happened.''

Michael didn't believe her for a moment, but he couldn't force her to talk to him. He shoved his hands into the pockets of his suit pants. ''You'll call me if you need anything?''

''Of course. Thank you.'' She turned away, flipping the lock open. It was dismissal, polite but firm, and there was no arguing with it. Michael turned, taking a step away, every instinct screaming that all was not right, that he shouldn't leave her like this.

He turned back, uncertain of what he was going to say but knowing he had to speak up. Only it wasn't necessary. Hearing him approach, Brittany started to turn from the half-open door. She stopped, wavered and lifted a hand to her forehead, her skin suddenly dead white. Michael caught her as her knees buckled.

She sagged against him, unconscious. He lifted her into his arms, feeling his heart jump with fear. She was so pale. Pushing the door open with his shoulder, he carried her inside, kicking the door shut behind him. They were in the living room, a plain room with furniture that looked as if it had been moved in when the house was built and hadn't been shifted so much as an inch since.

Carrying Brittany to the sofa, set rigidly in place between two end tables, Michael laid her down. She stirred, moaning faintly. Not knowing what else to do, he crouched next to her, taking her hand in his, patting it gently. Her lashes lifted slowly, and she stared at him, dazed.

"You fainted."

"Did I?" she asked, lifting her free hand to touch her forehead, as if not sure that either still belonged to her.

"I think I should call a doctor."

"No!" Her fingers tightened over his, her eyes frightened. "I don't need a doctor."

"Brittany, you fainted."

"It's been a rough day." She struggled up, obviously determined to put the incident behind her. Michael helped her sit up and then sat next to her, still holding her hand.

"You're as pale as a ghost, and your pulse is faster than it should be."

She tugged her hand from his, shooting him a resentful look from under sooty lashes. "I thought you were an architect, not a doctor."

"I thought I was a friend."

"You are, Michael. You know you are." She was distressed that he would think otherwise.

"Then why won't you tell me what's troubling you?"

"Because, there are some things that you just can't help with."

"Try me." A vague suspicion was forming in the back of his mind.

"I can't," she whispered, shaking her head.

"Brittany." He stopped, staring at her bent head. This was none of his business. She was Dan's girl. But as Dan's best friend, didn't he have an obligation to look after her? Isn't that what Dan would have wanted? But if she didn't want his help... In the end, it wasn't a matter of logical argument. He simply couldn't leave her like this.

"Brittany, are you pregnant?"

She jumped as if he'd cracked a lash across her shoulders, her head jerking up, wide gray eyes meeting his.

"No, of course not." But the truth was in her eyes, and Michael felt a hardness in his chest that was impossible to define.

"Did Dan know?" he asked tightly. If Dan had known and left her alone...

"I told you, I'm not—" She broke off, reading the hopelessness of the lie in his look. Her shoulders slumped and she dropped her gaze to her clasped hands. "No. He didn't know."

Michael drew in a deep breath. Dan hadn't known. The idea that he could have known and abandoned Brittany had been insupportable.

"You didn't know?" he questioned.

"I knew. I should have told him. If I had, maybe he wouldn't have gone, and he'd still be alive." She waved a hand, forestalling his protest. "I know it's stupid to think that way, but I can't help it."

Michael reached out, catching her hand in his. "Why didn't you tell him?"

"We fought. I wanted to get married, and he said it was stupid to get married while I was still in school. He said we'd talk about it when he got back. Only now he won't be coming back," she ended starkly.

"If you'd told him..."

"I know. I know. If I'd told him I was pregnant, he'd have married me. But then how would I ever know if he married me because he wanted to or because he *had* to?"

"Dan was crazy about you," Michael protested.

"Maybe. But I'd never have known for sure."

There didn't seem to be anything to say. Michael stared at their linked hands. What was he supposed to do now? What would Dan have wanted him to do?

"What are you going to do now?" he asked finally, feeling hopelessly inadequate.

"I don't know. There hasn't been much time to think since I got the news about Dan."

He stood up, moving away restlessly. "Are you going to have the baby?" The question came out too abruptly, and he shook his head. "Forget it. It's none of my business."

"It's all right." Now that the truth was out, Brittany seemed much more calm. "I'm going to have it. This is my child, mine and Dan's." Her fingers touched her still-flat stomach as if she could feel the tiny life she carried. "It's a part of us—all that's left, in a way."

"Is there anything I can do?" he asked, feeling awkward and uncertain. "Anything you need?"

"No. I'm going to be just fine." She lifted her chin, drawing her shoulders straight. "I fell apart today, but that won't happen again."

"Are you sure? Anything at all. I'm not just asking because you're carrying Dan's baby."

She half smiled but shook her head again. "Thank you. After the way I dissolved all over you, I'm surprised you didn't run for cover ages ago."

"Today was rough for all of us," he said.

"I know. I don't know what I'd have done without you. Thank you, Michael."

"No big deal." He shrugged her thanks away. He didn't want her gratitude.

"It was a big deal to me." She stood up and crossed

the short distance between them. Michael looked down into her eyes, feeling an odd wariness he couldn't quite define. She raised up on her toes, balancing herself with a hand on his arm as she placed a kiss on his cheek.

Her mouth felt soft on his beard-roughened skin. Her scent was soft also, a mixture of lavender and sunshine. It drew him, making him want to put his arms around her and bury his face in her hair. Maybe then he could forget the aching sense of loss that gnawed at him. With Brittany in his arms, surely anything would be possible.

The feeling was so strong that he took a step back, the movement too quick so that she almost lost her balance. He put a hand to her waist, steadying her for an instant before withdrawing even that small contact.

It was safer if he didn't touch her. Safer in what way, he couldn't have said.

"You must be tired," he muttered.

"I am." If she noticed anything odd in his behavior, he couldn't tell. She pushed a straying lock of hair back.

"Your parents, they'll help you?"

"They'll be pretty upset, but I believe, when it comes right down to it, they'll do everything they can."

"Well, if there's any problem, call me."

"I will."

The pause threatened to grow awkward. He should leave. He'd said everything he could. She was probably hoping he'd go. But still he lingered, reluctant to leave her.

"Are you sure there isn't something I can do? There must be something you want or need."

"No, really Michael, I'm doing okay."

"You'll call me if you need anything?" He edged toward the door, torn between his concern and his need to put some distance between them.

"I'm not going to need anything."

"Promise you'll call me," he insisted again.

"I'll call you."

He reached out, unable to resist the urge to smooth back that errant lock of hair. "We're not going to lose touch," he told her firmly. "If you don't call me, I'm going to come looking for you."

"Okay." Tears trembled on her lashes, but she managed a wavering smile. "We won't lose touch."

Courting fire, he bent and kissed her cheek. When his head lifted, their eyes met for a long, silent moment before he turned and left without looking back.

Long strides carried him down the walkway, but once in the Mustang, he just sat, staring out the windshield. A vague headache throbbed behind his eyes. The days since the news had come about the plane crash blurred together in one indistinguishable gray fog. The memorial service was already half-forgotten.

Dan was gone. It was a fact that had to be accepted. Only Dan wasn't really gone. Brittany was carrying his child. The headache intensified. He should be glad that something of his friend would continue in the world. So why was it that all he could think of was that if Dan were to appear in front of him right at this moment, alive and unhurt, his first urge would be to punch him in the teeth?

# Chapter Two

Brittany watched Michael go, feeling as if a lifeline were vanishing. After shutting the door behind him, she had to bite her lip to keep from calling him back.

"Don't be stupid," she muttered to herself. She didn't have anything to worry about. She was young and healthy. The doctor had told her that there was no reason to expect any problems with the pregnancy. Lots of women went through a pregnancy alone these days. There was no reason in the world why she should cling to Michael Sinclair.

She sat down, linking her hands together in her lap, fingers tense. She was going to be fine. The low growl of the Mustang's engine brought her to her feet. Standing at the window, she watched as it pulled away from the curb and disappeared down the street. She bit her lip, weak tears filling her eyes. He was gone. She hadn't realized how desperately she'd wanted him to come back. His arms had felt so strong, as if he could protect her from anything.

For the first time since Dan left, she'd felt secure.

The future hadn't seemed quite so frightening. She'd tried to be positive with Michael, telling him that everything was going to be all right. What she desperately needed was someone to convince her of that.

Brushing impatiently at the dampness on her cheeks, she drew in a deep breath, then she turned away from the window and the empty street outside. She was behaving like a die-away heroine in a Victorian novel. She'd felt safe with Michael Sinclair, but that was probably because he reminded her of Dan. Not that the two men were anything alike, but they'd been best friends. Being with Michael almost made her feel as if Dan couldn't be far away.

Dan. Tears filled her eyes again. It just wasn't possible that he wasn't coming back. He'd always been so vibrant, so strong. Not the kind of quiet strength Michael had. Dan's had been a more boisterous, outgoing kind of strength.

Michael seemed to think things out before he acted. Dan hadn't thought anything out. He'd been quick to laugh as much as he'd been quick to anger—whichever, he was always gloriously alive.

If only she'd told him about the baby that last night. If he'd known she was pregnant, he'd never have left her. But she hadn't told him. Her stupid pride had demanded that he want to marry her without knowing about the child. They'd quarreled, then Dan had stormed off for Los Angeles, where the team was gathering. He'd never known about the baby. She'd thought that there'd be time to tell him, time to make up. Only they'd run out of time.

Brittany rested her hand on her flat stomach. The child she carried was all she had left of him. There was no outward sign yet, but she could feel the changes in her body. Inside, a new life was growing, one that would be a part of her and Dan and yet wholly its own. She didn't have time to wallow in grief and self-pity. She had to go on. Dan would have expected it of her, and more importantly, she owed it to the child—her and Dan's.

She reached out to straighten a doily on an end table. There was no sense in dwelling on the past. It couldn't be changed. The future was what counted now. And she had the best reason in the world to focus on the future.

Glancing at the clock, she figured her parents would be home soon. They'd gone to the golf course as they had every Thursday afternoon since her father retired. They didn't know about the baby, barely even knew about Dan. She'd tell them this afternoon.

She'd given a lot of thought to the future—her future and her child's. It wouldn't be easy, but she thought she could manage the first semester of the year during her pregnancy. After that, she'd have to take some time off. But once the baby was a few months old, she could finish school, get her degree and then get her teaching credentials.

Once she got a job, she'd be able to start creating a home for herself and her son or daughter. Her plan would work. She knew it would. But it was going to require a lot of help from her parents. She could count on them—couldn't she? Despite her determination to stay positive, she felt a chill. They weren't likely to take the news well.

Like the house, her parents hadn't changed with the times. She'd been born late in both their lives, a not entirely welcome surprise. They'd done their best, but their lives had already been neatly and precisely established when she was born, and they hadn't seen any reason to make more than the absolutely necessary changes.

Brittany had always accepted the fact that she was somewhat of an intruder in her parents' lives. It wasn't that they didn't care about her. It was simply that there wasn't really a place for her. In a way, she admired them. The rest of the world might be embracing flexible morals and ethics that could be tailored to any situation, but in the Winslow household, right was still right and wrong was always wrong. Things were black-and-white, never muddy gray.

Good people went to church on Sunday, voted in every election and minded their own business. Men held jobs and supported their families. Women stayed home and raised the children.

They'd reluctantly conceded that perhaps the world had changed somewhat in this respect. It might not be a bad idea for a woman to have a way to earn a living, which was why they'd agreed to finance her education. Brittany suspected it was the thought of having her dependent on them that had swayed them.

One thing she was sure they hadn't changed their views on was that a good girl did not sleep with a man before marriage. She'd half agreed with them until she met Dan. With Dan everything had been different.

She sighed, wrapping her arms around her waist. She had to tell her parents about this. She needed their support, financially and emotionally. They loved her. They might be hurt, disappointed in her, even, but they'd be able to set that aside. Wouldn't they?

"How could you do something like this?" It was her father who spoke, but looking from one accusing

face to the other, Brittany knew that it could have come
from either of them.

"It wasn't something I planned, Dad. It just happened."

"This sort of thing doesn't 'just happen' to girls who
don't do things they shouldn't." That was her mother,
her plain features drawn into distressed lines as she
looked at her daughter.

"Mom, I—" She broke off, searching for words.
How did she explain her relationship with Dan, that
being with him had seemed the most right thing in the
world? Her mother couldn't even say the word *sex*, let
alone understand the needs she'd felt in Dan's arms.
Brittany had often thought her own conception a miracle.

"What about the father? Is he willing to do the right
thing by you?" her father demanded sternly.

The question sent a stabbing pain through her, and
it was a moment before she could answer. The loss
was still so fresh.

"I told you, Dad. Dan died in a plane crash last
week," she said quietly. *How could they have forgotten
that?* "If he were here, yes, I think he'd want to marry
me."

"You *think* he'd want to marry you?" Her father
glared at her from the depths of his wing chair. "You
*think*? You did *that*—" his tone made the simple word
an obscenity "—with a boy whom you only *thought*
would marry you?"

Brittany immediately felt as if she'd been branded
with a scarlet letter. *S* for slut. Color rose in her cheeks,
and her eyes stung.

"Things are different now, Dad. It isn't considered
a crime to sleep with a man before you get married.

And I love...loved Dan." She bit her lip against the pain of using the past tense.

"Things aren't different in this household, young lady. I thought we'd raised you to a better standard than that. That's the trouble with the world today. Too many young people going out and doing just what they want to do without a thought to right or wrong."

"George, I think it's best if we don't get distracted from the matter at hand." His wife pulled him away from a lecture Brittany had heard many times in the past. "We need to decide what we're going to do about her."

"*Her?*" Brittany said. "You don't have talk about me as if I'm deaf, Mom." She tried a wavering smile, but her hand was clenched on the arm of the sofa.

This wasn't what she'd expected. This attitude that she'd committed a capital crime. She'd known that they'd be disappointed, angry, hurt, but she hadn't been prepared for the coldness. My God, they were looking at her as if they disliked her.

"I'm sorry if I've hurt you. I never intended to hurt you. But I need your support now. More than ever before."

Despite the naked plea in her voice, there was no warming in the eyes turned toward her, and a cold lump of fear settled in the pit of her stomach.

"Our 'support'?" her mother questioned. "How can we support what you've done?"

"It's not like I killed anybody. I made a mistake."

"I think the problem, Brittany, is that you think the mistake is in turning up like this...." Her father waved his hand in her direction, unable or unwilling to say the actual word. "The real mistake was in being...

intimate with this young man to start with. This is your punishment for your immoral actions.''

Brittany stared at him as if seeing him for the first time. How could he sit there and pass judgment on her like this?

"I don't think I want to think of my baby as a punishment for my—actions."

"Perhaps not, but that's what it is," her mother said.

"So what's the bottom line here?" Brittany asked, anger lending a challenging edge to her voice. "Are you going to cast me from your home, refuse to acknowledge my existence?"

"Certainly not." Ann Winslow arranged her full skirt more neatly around her knees, fussing with it until it fell into precise folds. "Your father and I would never do such a thing."

Brittany drew a deep breath, feeling the tears—so quick these days—start to her eyes. For a moment she'd been facing a very bleak future.

"I knew I could count on you."

"Naturally. We *are* your parents. We've always done our best by you. You have no reason to think that we wouldn't this time, also."

"Thank you. I know this is very hard for both of you."

"It would have been nice if you'd thought of that before you did what you did," her father said repressively.

Brittany bit her tongue, holding back the urge to tell him that this might just be a little harder on her than it was on them.

"George, there's no sense in recriminations now. What's done is done."

Brittany allowed some of the tension to ease from

her muscles. It was going to be all right. They were upset. It had been foolish of her not to realize just how upset they'd be. But it was going to be all right now. They'd had a chance to absorb the shock. Her mother would calm her father's indignation, and they'd work things out. It might be a while before they forgave her completely, but once they saw their grandchild, all this would seem so unimportant.

"What's important now is to decide just how we're going to handle this." Brittany brought her attention back to the conversation as her mother continued, the relief making her feel almost light-headed.

"I'd like to finish college," she said. "I know it won't be easy, what with the baby due in the middle of the school year, but I think it's important."

"Brittany, please don't interrupt. This is something your father and I will have to give some consideration."

"Isn't my input important?" Her half smile went unanswered, and a small chill settled in her chest. Things were going to be all right, weren't they?

"I believe you have already proved that your judgment is less than sound," her mother said coolly. "I suggest you let your father and I come to some decisions regarding your future."

"Since *we* are discussing *my* future, I'd like some say in any decisions that are made."

"Very well. Your father and I haven't had a chance to discuss it yet, of course, but I think the appropriate path is quite clear. You should go to your aunt and uncle in New York. They have a house in the upstate area, and I'm sure they won't mind having you stay with them.

"You can stay there until the child is born, at which

time it can be put up for adoption, then you can come home.''

Brittany heard the last words as if they were coming to her through a long tunnel. She lifted a hand to her throat, her fingers were shaking.

"You're not serious," she finally managed to get out.

"Certainly I'm serious," her mother said, as if what she'd proposed wasn't the most horrible thing Brittany had ever heard in her life.

"This is my child you're talking about. Your grandchild."

"This child is an embarrassment to the family," her father said. "What would the neighbors say?"

"'What would the neighbors say?'" Brittany repeated incredulously. "You're actually worried about what the neighbors might think?"

"Naturally. We have to live among these people."

"And what they think is more important to you than your grandchild. You're more concerned with their opinions than the fact that the man I was in love with is dead."

"Don't be melodramatic, Brittany." That was her mother, her tone soothing. "Naturally, we're very sorry that he's dead."

"But only because he can't make an honest woman of me now. Right?" Brittany shot to her feet. She felt as if she were seeing her parents for the first time. Their narrow little world was no longer just an odd quirk— it was a smothering reality. It had choked the life out of them a long time ago, and now it was threatening to reach out and swallow her. "The truth is that you don't care about anything quite as much as you care about what other people might think.

"Well, I'll solve your problem for you. I'll go away. But I'm not going to hide my shame two thousand miles away. I'm not ashamed of what I did, and I'm not ashamed of my child. We'll manage just fine without you."

She turned and stalked from the room, ignoring her mother's startled look and her father's command that she come back. Taking the stairs two at a time, she sought the thin sanctuary of the room she'd had since childhood, slamming the door shut. She leaned back against the door, her heart pounding as if she'd run a marathon.

How could they talk like that? Look at her like that? This was a child she was carrying, not an embarrassment to be quickly swept under the carpet. Didn't they have any feeling for the baby? For her?

She wrapped her arms around her middle, suddenly feeling very cold. All her life she'd been the intruder in their lives, the interruption they hadn't planned or truly welcomed. And she'd accepted that. They loved her in their own way, perhaps not as she'd have wished but as much as they were capable of. She'd never doubted that.

Now, she was seeing how foolish she'd been. They didn't love her. They couldn't. If they loved her, they could never have sat there talking to her like that, suggesting that she give her baby away as if it were an unwanted bundle.

She didn't have to stay here. She *wouldn't* stay. She would go somewhere else, build a life for herself and her son or daughter. Determination carried her as far as dragging her suitcase from the closet. As she placed it on the bed, the reality of her predicament began to set in.

Just where was she supposed to go?

She sat down next to the open suitcase, staring at it blankly. She had some money but only a few hundred dollars. The new school year seemed so far away. The friend she roomed with then was in Boston with her relatives, and they'd sublet their tiny apartment for the summer. Even if Janie was around, she couldn't support the two of them.

There was a baby on the way. Having babies was not cheap. She'd counted on the fact that her father's insurance might cover the hospital costs. And after the baby was born, what was she going to live on then?

Tears burned her eyes, but she blinked them back. She'd cried enough today, cried enough to last a lifetime. Tears weren't going to solve any of her problems. She couldn't stay here. That much was clear. It was also clear that there'd be no going back to college in the fall.

She got up and moved to the dresser, grabbing a handful of lingerie at random. Dropping it into the suitcase, she moved to the closet, lifting out a stack of hangers. In a few months, none of her clothes would fit her. Where was the money going to come from for new ones?

A soft tapping at the door interrupted the panicked circle of her thoughts. She stiffened, staring at the door warily.

"Yes?"

"Brittany, I'd like to talk to you." Her mother's voice was muffled. Brittany hesitated. The pain she'd felt downstairs was still fresh. If her mother was going to try to talk her into giving up her baby, she didn't want to hear it. On the other hand, maybe they'd realized what a mistake they were making.

"Come in."

She didn't look at her mother as the door opened and then shut. Carrying the stack of clothes to the bed, she began stripping them from the hangers, folding them as neatly as her shaking hands would allow, conscientiously arranging them in the suitcase.

"You're leaving."

"You don't expect me to stay here, do you?"

"Where are you going?"

"I don't know. A motel for a day or two until I can figure out what to do. Do you care as long as the neighbors don't find out I'm pregnant?" Her eyes met her mother's challengingly, and Ann's dropped first.

"Naturally, I care. You *are* my daughter."

"What would people think if you didn't care?" Brittany said with a sudden flash of insight. Harsh spots of color appeared in her mother's thin cheeks, and she didn't lift her eyes. Brittany hadn't thought she could be hurt any more, but she felt a sharp stab of pain at the guilt she read in her mother's silence.

"Oh, Mom. Is that why you came up here? Because you're worried about what your friends will think if you don't try to talk me out of this?"

"Of course not." But the denial came a little too late to be completely believable. She lifted her head, reading the accusation in Brittany's eyes, her flush deepening. "You act as if what people think of you isn't important. That's easy to believe at your age. When you get a little older, you realize that people's opinions can reflect on every aspect of your life—the kind of job you can get, where you live, who your friends are. If people don't think well of you, respect you, then life isn't very pleasant."

Brittany looked at her mother and felt a deep pity.

All these years she'd thought that maybe there was something wrong with her that her parents couldn't love her the way other people loved their children. But it hadn't been her at all.

"I didn't say that it isn't important to consider other people's opinions," she said gently. "But you can't live your life by them. There are things that have to come before that, things like love and family."

For a moment she thought she saw a flicker of uncertainty in her mother's eyes, as if maybe she was getting through. Mother and daughter faced each other across a chasm so wide neither could quite see how to cross it. There was a moment, a moment only, when they almost reached out, but then Ann looked away, and Brittany knew then that nothing had changed. Maybe it was too late for her mother to change.

"Naturally, you're entitled to your opinion. Your father and I have tried to be good parents. We cannot do more than that."

"No, I guess you can't." Brittany went to the closet and reached for another handful of hangers, tears blurring her vision. She carried the clothes back to the bed and began pulling them off the hangers, folding them roughly and stuffing them into the suitcase. Her mother watched silently, obviously feeling that she should say something or do something and obviously at a total loss as to what.

"We only want what's best for you, Brittany," she tried at last. "You think we're being very harsh, but a child is an enormous responsibility."

"Well, you don't have to worry about that. It will be my responsibility, not yours." Brittany swept a handful of bottles off the dresser, dumping them in on top of her clothes with a rattle of glass.

"If you're determined to do this, there's nothing we can do to stop you."

"I'm determined."

The flat answer seemed to leave her mother momentarily without words. "At least wait until morning. Sleep on this decision."

"I don't need to sleep on it." She pushed the top of the suitcase closed and flipped the latches.

"Wait until morning, anyway. It's getting dark. There's no sense in you trying to find a place to stay tonight."

Brittany's first instinct was to refuse to spend another minute under this roof, but she hesitated. The events of the day had been more than a little draining. She was running on adrenaline now, but she knew that when it faded, exhaustion was going to hit her. She got tired so much quicker these days. Besides, if she stayed here tonight, she could save the money a motel would cost her. Pride had its place, but she had more than herself to consider now.

She nodded slowly. "All right. I'll wait till morning." She dragged the suitcase off the bed, setting it on the floor with a thump before turning to look at her mother. "I'm not changing my mind about this. But you're right, it would be foolish to leave now. I'll stay tonight."

"Good." Ann nodded briskly, turning to leave. She stopped, her hand on the doorknob, her back to her daughter. "It's not that I don't care, you know." Her voice was so low, Brittany had to strain to hear it.

"I know." That seemed to be all her mother needed. She left the room, closing the door behind her, leaving Brittany to stare at the blank panel of wood.

She felt numb. The day had been full of too much

emotion, too much stress. She was physically and mentally exhausted. She wanted to crawl into bed and pull the covers over her head. She wanted to cry and scream and demand that somebody make things right again. But there was nobody who could. Most of all, she wanted somebody to lean on, just for a little while. But there was nobody for that, either.

Except Michael Sinclair.

The thought popped into her head unbidden. Michael had been there for her this afternoon. For a few wonderful moments, she hadn't been so completely alone. He'd been Dan's best friend. She could call him. He'd come get her, find her a place to stay. She knew he'd help her.

But what right did she have to drag him into this? True, he'd said to call him if she needed anything, but that was one of those polite gestures people made, never expecting you to take them up on it. Remembering those dark blue eyes, she found it hard to believe that Michael Sinclair ever said anything he didn't mean.

Still, even if he *had* meant it, he'd been thinking in terms of something small. She couldn't call him up and tell him she needed money, a place to stay and a job, and gee, could he do anything about it?

Pride forbade it.

She couldn't afford pride right now. Or was it that pride was all she could afford?

She rubbed at the ache in her temples. She was so tired. Kicking off her shoes, she turned back the covers, crawling under them fully dressed. She'd just lie down for a few minutes. When she woke up, things would be more clear.

The pillow had never felt softer as her head sank

into it. She couldn't remember ever being so achingly tired. The memorial service, the scene with her parents, the aching loss that nagged at her heart, all blurred into a gray fog as her eyes drifted shut. Just a little rest and she'd feel much better.

She fell asleep with her thoughts still a tangled mess. She dreamed—vague, amorphous dreams in which the only thing that was clear was the presence of a tall man with tobacco-brown hair and eyes the color of a summer sky. In the dreams, he held her close, protecting her from the shadows that tugged at her. And she felt safe.

# Chapter Three

Michael slowed the Mustang to a near crawl as he turned the corner onto the quiet street. He still wasn't sure about the wisdom of coming here. He should have just called. He could have found out how Brittany was doing over the phone.

But he wanted to see her. If he was honest with himself, he'd been wanting to see her since about thirty seconds after he'd walked out the door after the memorial service. He'd been fighting the urge for weeks, and he'd finally lost the battle.

He pulled up to the curb in front of the house and got out. It was early October now; the trees, though still green, were beginning to look worn and pale. It wouldn't be long before they'd start turning, then the leaves would fall, a soft prelude to winter's snow.

The neighborhood was as overly structured as it had been the first time he saw it. He hunched his shoulders beneath the soft flannel shirt, feeling constricted. Everything was so tidy, so square. Each house aligned precisely with the ones beside it. Each path leading directly from the street to the front door.

Shoving his hands into the pockets of his jeans, he stared at the house in front of him. He should have called or come to see her ages ago. There hadn't been a day when he hadn't thought about her, wondered how she was doing.

The very intensity of his desire had kept him away. Brittany had been Dan's girl. When it came right down to it, he didn't even know her all that well. Maybe his desire to see her was some tangled way of trying to hold on to Dan. And maybe it wasn't.

He muttered a curse under his breath as he started up the walkway. He didn't normally spend this much time analyzing his reasons for doing something. And he was an idiot to do it this time. He was concerned about Brittany because his best friend had been in love with her, was the father of the child she carried. There was nothing wrong with wanting to make sure she was all right. He was doing this for Dan, that's all.

His boot heels echoed on the wooden porch, announcing his presence even before he rang the doorbell. He could hear the bell ringing inside the house, a dignified two-tone sound as dull and uninspired as the neighborhood.

"So what did you expect, 'Yankee Doodle Dandy'?" he muttered under his breath.

The woman who opened the door bore enough resemblance to Brittany to make their relationship apparent. Her hair was streaked with gray, but the color underneath was the same deep black as her daughter's. Her eyes were gray, also like Brittany's, but it was a dull color, not the warm shade that made Brittany's so striking.

"Mrs. Winslow?"

She eyed him through the screen without warmth. "Yes."

"I'm Michael Sinclair. I'm a friend of Brittany's." That got a flicker of reaction, but it wasn't welcome.

"Yes." There was nothing added to the single syllable. Michael drew a deep breath, wondering if there was something wrong with the woman.

"Is Brittany here?" He tried a smile, but it didn't seem to help.

"No, she's not."

Something more than one syllable. They were making progress.

"Do you expect her soon? I'd like to talk to her."

The pause stretched until he began to think she wasn't going to answer.

"She doesn't live here anymore."

"She's moved out?" He felt a twinge of uneasiness. It seemed an odd time for her to be moving out, unless... "Did she go back to school?"

"I couldn't say." The flat statement was not encouraging, but he tried anyway.

"I don't mean to be rude, but I really would like to see her. I'm not an insurance salesman or anything. I was a friend of Dan's."

This time there was no mistaking the chill in her eyes. "If you wish to see her, you'll have to look for her. I'm afraid I can't help you. Good day."

The door shut quietly but firmly, leaving him staring at it. He waited, half expecting it to open again, unable to believe that the conversation had been concluded so abruptly. But the door didn't open. After a moment, he turned and walked off the porch, going over the conversation in his mind, trying to find a reason for the hostility she'd clearly felt.

There'd been caution when she opened the door, which was understandable. Even in Remembrance, people were a little hesitant to open their door to a stranger these days. When he'd said he wanted to see Brittany, the caution had taken on an uneasy edge. It was Dan's name that had seemed to bring out the hostility.

Michael frowned as he slid into the Mustang. He supposed he could understand why Brittany's parents would feel some anger toward Dan. He'd left her alone and pregnant. Even though it was hardly his fault that he hadn't come back, maybe her parents couldn't be expected to see the more logical side of the situation.

He started the engine and pulled away from the curb. But her mother had acted as if she didn't even know where Brittany was. At a time like this, wouldn't she have wanted to stay near her family? Surely she'd need their support, in more ways than one.

If she wasn't with her family, where was she? She could have gone back to school. Maybe her mother was the secretive type and hadn't wanted to tell him where Brittany was.

He braked at the light on Main, his eyes unfocused as he waited for the light to change. There was an uneasy feeling in the pit of his stomach, a feeling that something wasn't right. If Brittany was in trouble, wouldn't she have called him? But why should she? He hadn't called her all these months; she probably thought he wouldn't want to hear from her.

The driver behind him tapped his horn impatiently. Michael blinked, realizing that the light was green and had been for some seconds. He turned right and then coasted the car to a stop next to the curb, oblivious to the fact that he was in a red zone. He wasn't parking, anyway; he was thinking. He left the engine idling, his fingers tapping on the wheel.

Ten to one, Brittany was fine. She'd probably think it was pretty peculiar if he went to a lot of trouble to find her. But what if she wasn't fine, as his instincts were screaming? He had to know. If he had to justify it, then he owed it to Dan to make sure she was all right.

So how was he going to find out if his instincts were right? Her parents were a dead end. They either genuinely didn't know, which he found appalling, or they weren't going to tell him.

If Brittany had gone back to school, she'd probably gone back to the little apartment she'd shared with that other student. What was her name? He'd only met her once, a pretty girl with red hair. Jenny? Gerry? Janie. That was it. Janie. She was probably safe and sound with Janie.

He glanced at the wide gold watch on his wrist, a frown hooking his dark brows together. He was supposed to be on the Adams site in less than an hour. His parents had come back from their cruise weeks ago and Donovan was back in the office, but the Adams project was his design and his responsibility.

When he got back to the office this afternoon, he could see if there was a phone listed under Brittany's name in Indianapolis. And if there wasn't? The phone could be in her roommate's name, though he hadn't the slightest idea what Janie's last name was. He knew where they lived. He'd gone with Dan once to pick Brittany up, and he knew he could find the apartment again.

Was he actually thinking of driving into the city just because he felt a little uneasy? Brittany would think he was crazy if he showed up on her doorstep out of the blue. He'd call her this afternoon. If he couldn't find her number, *then* he'd think about the next step.

He flipped on his turn signal, watching for a break in traffic before pulling out. Maybe Dan's death had left him a little paranoid. There was no reason why Brittany should have kept in touch with him, no reason why he should feel this knot in his stomach.

Approaching the highway, he moved into the right lane. He'd go out to the Adams site, talk with the foreman, meet with the inspector and do all the things an architect was supposed to do. When he got back to the office, he'd get Brittany's number and give her a call, then he could see how foolish he'd been to worry. That was the only sane, logical thing to do.

Horns blared behind him as he abruptly switched lanes, gunning the engine to cut through a gap in traffic and turn left onto the highway. He could call the site from the city and reschedule. First, he had to know that Brittany was all right. He lowered his foot on the accelerator.

Finding the apartment wasn't hard. It wasn't a large building or particularly elegant, but it was well kept and close to the university. It was the latter attribute that guaranteed the owners a full roster of tenants.

He parked down the street from the building. Now that he was here, he felt like an idiot. He'd canceled a business appointment and made a two-hour drive without a shred of evidence that there was anything to worry about. He wasn't even sure what he was going to say to Brittany once he saw her. *Just happened to be in the neighborhood and thought I'd drop by?*

Not too likely. He could hardly tell her that he'd driven all this way just because he had a feeling that something was wrong. She'd think he was crazy. Which was exactly how he felt. He hunched his shoulders, glaring at the modest building as he approached. For two cents he'd turn around and go home. Except that he knew he wouldn't feel easy until he'd seen her, assured himself she was all right. It was the least he owed Dan, he told himself.

The apartment was upstairs, and he found himself measuring the stairs as he climbed, trying to judge how difficult they'd be for a pregnant woman to manage. He was not happy with the results. The steep stairs would be a hazard.

He frowned as he stepped out onto the landing and started down the hallway. The image of Brittany heavy with child brought mixed emotions that he still hadn't been able to sort out. Concern, he understood. The anger that tugged at him when he thought about the child she carried was something else again.

He stopped in front of the door, staring at the blank panel for a long moment before ringing the bell. He was just going to say hello, assure himself that she was doing fine, then he'd leave.

He waited and when no one came to the door, he rang the bell again. There was still no response. He leaned heavily on the bell, though it was obvious that nobody was home. In all his mental arguments, he hadn't thought of the simple possibility that nobody would be here.

Now, faced with the unresponsive door, he was nonplussed. Should he leave a note or wait in the car until someone came home? Since the whole purpose of this visit was to assuage his overactive imagination, leaving a note was not going to do much good. On the other hand, sitting in the car like a lovesick teenager didn't hold much appeal, either.

He gave the bell one last irritated jab. This had started out earlier as a simple visit. He should have been on the Adams site hours ago instead of standing here in this drafty hallway feeling like an idiot. Disgusted, he turned from the door.

He was halfway to the stairs when he noticed the girl coming toward him. Even in the dimly lighted hall, that red hair was unmistakable.

"Janie?"

He spoke too loudly, his voice echoing in the hallway, and she jumped, dropping two books from the stack she carried. She looked at him warily, glancing over her shoulders as if judging the distance to the stairs.

"Sorry. I didn't mean to scare you," he apologized as he bent to scoop up the books. "Michael Sinclair. We met about six months ago. I'm... I was a friend of Dan Remington's."

The tension left her shoulders and she smiled, reaching out to take the books he was holding. "Sure. Sorry I didn't recognize you at first. The light in here is lousy. We keep nagging the manager, and she keeps saying she'll change it, but she never does." She was moving down the hall as she talked, digging in her purse for her keys. "Come on in."

Michael followed her into the apartment, pushing the door shut behind him. Janie dropped the stack of books on a table, then she kicked off her shoes before turning to look at him.

"I was really sorry to hear about Dan. I didn't know him all that well, but Brittany was crazy about him. Seems incredible, doesn't it?"

"Yes, it does." He wasn't here to discuss Dan. That wound was still too raw to bear any probing.

"I guess it just goes to prove that you can't count on anything. Can I get you something to drink? I've got some soda, milk if you're the healthy type, or there may be some cheap wine left over from the weekend, but you drink at your own risk."

"No, thanks." Michael reined in his impatience, but perhaps he didn't do a very good job. Janie glanced at him and grinned, her rather ordinary features lighting with amusement.

"I guess you didn't come all this way for idle chit-chat."

"Sorry. I didn't mean to be rude."

"Not rude, exactly. But you look like you might start pacing at any moment. To save wear and tear on the carpet, why don't we cut to the chase?" She leaned back against the breakfast counter, which separated the kitchen from the living room. "What can I do for you?"

"I'm looking for Brittany."

"I thought you might be. She isn't here."

"You mean she isn't home?"

"No, I mean she doesn't live here anymore." She hitched herself onto a tall stool, settling her feet on the top rung.

"When did she move out?"

"Right before classes started."

"Where is she? Is she all right?" The questions came out with a sharp edge. All the uneasiness he'd felt earlier returned a hundredfold.

Janie gave him a long look as if weighing how much to say. "She's all right. At least she was a couple of weeks ago, which was the last time I saw her."

"Why did she move out? Is she still going to school? Where is she living?" He fired the questions at her, leaning forward as if prepared to shake the answers loose.

"Slow down." She leaned her elbows on the counter behind her, cocking her head to one side. "I guess you really are concerned about her. She moved out because her parents refused to continue to pay her tuition. No, she's not going to school."

"Where is she?"

Janie told him and Michael's uneasiness blossomed into full-fledged panic. The area she'd named was not a part of town where anyone lived by choice, especially not a woman alone.

Janie shrugged. "I told her she could stay here. My parents would have coughed up enough to cover the full rent. But she refused. She found this dinky little room, insisting it would be just perfect for her and the baby. You do know about the baby, don't you?"

"I know." He thrust his fingers through his hair. "Why didn't she call me? She can't stay there. It's not safe."

"That's what I told her, but she can be pretty stubborn."

"Stubborn? This isn't stubborn. This is insane. I need the address." There was an edge of anger in his voice that boded ill for Brittany when he found her.

Janie grinned as she turned and lifted a basket off the counter, shuffling through the stacks of paper that filled it to overflowing. "I tried to talk her out of it. Here it is."

Michael snatched the paper from her fingers, unconcerned with manners. "Thanks."

"I was going to copy it down for you," she commented mildly as he stuffed the paper into his shirt pocket. "That way I could keep it in my address file." She lifted the basket.

"You're not going to need it, because she's not going to be staying there."

"Well, I wish you better luck than I had in talking her out of it."

"I'll carry her out bodily if I have to," he promised. "Thanks for the help."

"You're welcome." But she was talking to the door as it shut behind him. She stared after him for a moment, a slow grin widening her mouth. She had the feeling that things were looking up for Brittany.

Michael found the address without trouble. If he'd considered it, he might have thought it a miracle that he could even read street signs through the fog of anger that all but blinded him.

What the hell was she thinking of? He parked the Mustang next to the curb, wedging it between two cars whose bodies were so rust pocked it was a miracle they didn't simply dissolve into piles of dust. Half a dozen children ranging from six to thirteen or so stopped their desultory game of kickball to stare at the shiny black car.

Michael noticed their interest and paused. At this point, he couldn't have cared if they stripped the car to the frame. On the other hand, it would delay his plans to get Brittany out of here immediately. He waved the oldest child over, a lanky boy with a shock of white-blond hair and a face much too old for his years.

"How would you like to earn fifty bucks?" The boy's eyes lighted with interest, but life had already taught him caution.

"Doin' what?"

"Keep an eye on my car for me. I'm going to be in there for a while. And if my car is still here and untouched when I come out, there's fifty bucks in it for you."

The boy's eyes flickered over the car. "I could get more than that for the hubcaps."

"Yeah, but then you'd have me to deal with." Their eyes met, each measuring the other. Finally, the boy nodded slowly.

"Okay. But how do I know you've even got fifty on you or that you'll give it to me when you come out?"

"So young, yet so suspicious," Michael chided, reaching for his wallet.

"Just practical, mister."

Michael pulled a fifty-dollar bill out of his wallet, tearing it neatly in two. He handed the boy one half and tucked the other back into his wallet. The boy looked at the half bill, then grinned.

"That's a pretty neat trick, mister. This won't do me no good if your car is gone. I'll take care of it for you."

"Thanks." Michael turned away, the momentary distraction forgotten as he walked up the cracked steps and pushed open the door of the apartment building. The entryway smelled of urine and despair. The carpeting was worn to the bare floor in places, creating traps for unwary feet. A row of brass-colored mail boxes lined one wall, the doors on several standing drunkenly open.

A steep flight of stairs rose along the left wall, and Michael picked his way over to them. An old man slept on the bottom stairs, hardly more than a bundle of rags and bones.

Michael's anger mounted with every step he took. The thought of Brittany living in a place like this was intolerable. Why hadn't she called him? She must have known he'd do anything to help her, anything at all.

*How could she have known, you jerk? You didn't get in touch with her.* He stepped around a carton whose contents had seeped onto the second-floor landing. Well, he was here now, and he wasn't leaving until he took Brittany with him. She wasn't spending another night in this place, not even if he had to drag her bodily from it.

Four doors faced onto the landing, each more battered than the last. He was unsurprised to find that Brittany's door was the most battle scarred, though it looked as if someone had made an effort to wash the worst of the grime from the peeling surface.

He drew a deep breath, controlling the urge to simply kick the door in and snatch her away. He'd stay calm and rational. And if that didn't work, there was always kidnapping.

He rapped on the door, the sound echoing off the low ceiling. He heard the door behind him open, but he didn't turn. Her neighbors were welcome to their curiosity. He was about to knock again when he heard a stir of sound from inside and then Brittany's voice, hesitant and holding a note of fear.

"Who is it?"

Relief surged through him, stealing his voice for an instant. Until he heard her voice, he hadn't realized just how much he'd feared that something might have happened to her. He cleared his throat.

"It's Michael." There was a long silence.

"Michael?" Her voice came from just the other side of the door. "Michael Sinclair?"

"No, Michael the ax murderer," he said drily. "Open the door, Brittany."

"I... Just a second." He heard her fumbling with the locks, and then the door opened slowly. She stood there, looking at him, her eyes uncertain, as if she could hardly believe that he was there.

Michael couldn't have believed that she could be even more beautiful than he remembered, but she was. She was paler, a little thinner. Dark circles created smudgy patterns under her eyes. But she was still hauntingly beautiful. His eyes skimmed over her, seeking reassurance that she'd come to no harm.

"Michael." She reached up, shoving the thick fall of her hair back self-consciously. "I wasn't expecting anybody. The place is a mess. *I'm* a mess."

"You look fine." He arched his brow questioningly when she continued to stand in the doorway. "Can I come in?"

"Oh. Sure. I'm sorry. I don't know where my manners are today." As she stepped back, he wondered if it was his imagination that she seemed reluctant to let him in. "Like I said, the place is a mess. Careful of that spot in the rug. It's inclined to trip people up."

Michael stepped over the torn place in the rug and into the living room. The apartment hadn't been an inspired creation when it was new. There were no interesting details to soften the boxy lines. Any charm it might once have had had been ground away by age and neglect.

One pane of window glass was broken and had been replaced with a sheet of plywood that looked as if it had been there for decades. The paint might once have been cream colored. Now it was a sad gray, showing too many years of wear.

The furniture was only marginally better. There was a sofa that sagged in the middle. Brittany had thrown colorful pillows over it, but nothing could disguise its age. Matchbooks propped up one leg of the scarred coffee table. An easy chair that looked as if it might or might not bear weight sat beside a lamp with a shade that had been wired into place.

Nothing Michael saw did anything to assuage the anger he felt at finding her here. He wanted to shake her. He wanted to snatch her up and carry her out of this place.

"Would you like something to drink?" She moved around him, fussing with the pillows on the sofa, picking up a blouse that had been draped over the back of it. "I guess you can tell I wasn't expecting anyone. The place never looks great, but it doesn't usually look this bad. I was going to clean house today. Not that there's a whole lot to clean." Still talking, she tossed the blouse through a door he assumed led to the bedroom.

"When in doubt, throw it in the bedroom. It's a good thing you can't see how bad it looks in there. I'm afraid my housekeeping skills only extend to the public areas. The bedroom always looks like a bomb just exploded in it. You never did say if you wanted something to drink. I don't know exactly what I have. Milk. I've been drinking so much milk I expect to start mooing any time now. There might be some soda. Janie brought some over last time she was here. Janie can't survive without soda. And I think I have some instant coffee. Of course, not everyone likes instant.''

"No, thank you.'' His words stopped her as she reached the kitchen door.

"'No, thank you'?''

"I don't want anything to drink.''

"Oh.''

His refusal seemed to leave her uncertain. She hovered in the doorway to the kitchen, looking as if she didn't know what to do. The silence stretched. Outside, children shouted in play. Someone started a car, the engine knocking and banging in protest. The smell of cooking onions drifted from somewhere nearby.

It was Michael who finally broke the silence.

"Why didn't you call me?''

*Why hadn't she called him?* Such a simple question. If only the answer was as simple. Brittany pleated the tail of her shirt, left out to conceal the fact that she could no longer button her jeans. Her fingers were trembling. She'd thought of calling him. There hadn't been a day that went by that she hadn't thought about it.

Now, seeing him here in this shabby room, she knew why she hadn't called. Pride. She'd wanted—needed—to do this on her own. Now that he was here, she knew she'd never been so glad to see anyone in her life. She sifted her hand through her hair, aware of the exhaustion that was never far away these days.

"I don't know,'' she answered him at last. "It's not really your problem, is it?''

"Not my problem,'' he repeated. "Did you think I wouldn't care?''

"No, of course not. I knew you'd care.''

"But you didn't call.''

"There was really no need. I'm managing all right."
He flicked a contemptuous look around the shabby
apartment, and she flushed. "Okay, so this is hardly a
Sinclair and Associates design, but it's not that bad."

"It's a pit," he said bluntly.

"How did you find me?" She couldn't argue with
his opinion, so she changed the subject.

"I went to see your parents." Her eyes flashed to
his, and though he wouldn't have thought it possible,
she seemed to pale a bit more. She looked away, staring at the faded carpeting.

"What did they say?" She poked at a threadbare
patch with her toe.

"Not much. I spoke with your mother...asked to see
you. She didn't seem to know where you were."

"I sent them my address. I bet they burned it for
fear the neighbors would find out where I was living."

There was a wealth of bitterness in her words, and
the picture Michael had been trying to piece together
became a little more clear.

"I gather they didn't take the news about the baby
very well."

She laughed but there was no humor in the sound.
"They wanted me to go off somewhere to have it and
then give it away. They were afraid that the *neighbors*
might find out about it."

"Why would the neighbors care?"

She laughed again, ending on a half sob. "That's the
funny thing. They wouldn't. But my parents are convinced that my having an illegitimate child—a bastard—could ruin them. Dammit" She scrubbed angrily
at the tears that spilled down her cheeks.

She looked so small, so forlorn and so proud. Michael wanted to take her in his arms and hold her, promise her that nothing was going to hurt her again.

Instead, he shoved his hands into his pockets, looking at the wall behind her, giving her a chance to compose herself.

"I'm sorry." She sniffed, wiping the moisture from her eyes. "It's not worth crying over."

"You should have called me."

"It wasn't your problem."

"I thought we were friends. And if that isn't enough, Dan was my best friend. That makes it my problem."

"Well, thank you." Her sarcastic tone made it clear that gratitude was not what she felt. Anger dried the last of her tears. "I'm so flattered to know that you consider me one of your problems."

"That's not the way I meant it."

"Just how did you mean it?" She tucked her hands into her pockets, her elbows hugging her sides. Just having him here created a roiling sensation in the pit of her stomach. She'd felt so many emotions since she'd heard his voice on the other side of the door—relief, joy, shame, anger. They were all tangled up inside. She wanted him to go away. She wanted him to stay. She wanted him to see that she could take care of herself. And she wanted him to put his arms around her and promise to take care of her.

"Look, I didn't mean to start a quarrel," Michael said. He thrust his fingers through his hair, his expression rueful. "I just don't understand why you'd choose to live like this—" his gesture encompassed the worn room "—when you must have known I'd gladly help you."

Her chin inched up a notch. "I've managed all right."

"Sure. You're doing just great. You're living in a building that should have been condemned ten years ago in a neighborhood Rocky would be afraid to walk through without an Uzi for protection. God knows what you're doing for money."

"My parents gave me the money they would normally have given me for my first quarter at school, and I've got a job."

"Doing what?"

"I'm a waitress at a perfectly respectable restaurant."

"What restaurant? That fleabag hangout down the street?" She didn't have to answer him. He could read it in her eyes. "Are you crazy? That place is probably frequented by every pimp and drug dealer within a fifteen-block radius. I bet you get more propositions than tips. And I suppose you walk there and back. Do you know what could happen to you on the street?"

"Nothing has happened to me." She knew it was a thin defense. The problem was that everything he was saying was true. It wasn't as though she hadn't had the same thoughts a hundred times herself. But it hadn't seemed as if she had a choice.

"You look like you haven't had a decent meal in weeks." Critical blue eyes raked her from head to foot. Brittany tugged defensively at her clothes.

"I've eaten."

"When? When did you eat last?"

"I...this morning," she finally got out. The truth was that she hadn't felt like eating for the past couple of days. Even as careful as she'd been, money was stretched thin. Worry and lack of sleep had drained her appetite.

"You're lying."

The flat statement stole her breath. She stared at him, searching for the words to protest, to argue, to say anything at all. He looked so angry. Why was he so angry with her? He was looking at her as if he hated her.

She blinked furiously against the tears that burned in her eyes. She wouldn't cry again. She would not cry. Pressing the back of her hand to her mouth, she struggled for control. She'd shed too many tears these past few weeks. But she lost the battle as the first salty drop found its way down her cheek. Furious with him, with herself, she turned away, holding her breath in an effort to grab hold of her dissolving control.

"I'm sorry." She hadn't heard him move, but suddenly he was right behind her, his hands on her shoulders. "I'm acting like a bastard. Don't cry, Brittany. I'm sorry."

If his anger had started her tears, it was his gentleness that caused them to overflow. Her breath left her on a sob as she bent to press her face into her hands.

"Damn." It was impossible to guess whether the mild curse was directed at her or at himself. She was beyond caring. When he turned her toward him, she didn't resist. It had been so long since she'd been able to lean on someone. She'd felt so abandoned and so scared.

She pressed her cheek against the soft flannel of his shirt. His arms were strong around her, just as she'd known they would be. For a little while, she could feel safe again.

Holding her, Michael fought to remember why he was here and just what the situation was. This was Brittany, his best friend's girl. She carried Dan's progeny. He was only holding her, comforting her because of Dan. He couldn't help Dan anymore, but he could make sure that the girl he'd loved, his child, were safe.

"Don't cry anymore. It's not good for you."

Brittany took a deep breath, choking off the next sob. It felt so good to lean on him, but she didn't have the right to do that. She drew a shuddering breath, pushing herself away, wiping at her eyes.

"I'm sorry." Half sobs broke the words. "I'm not usually such a crybaby. Hormones, I guess."

"I'm the one who should apologize." He handed her a handkerchief, watching as she dried her eyes and then blew her nose, a prosaic little gesture that seemed oddly touching. "I was a total bastard, and I'm sorry."

"Well, you weren't very nice," she agreed, staring at the handkerchief for a moment before stuffing it into her pocket.

"I had no business jumping all over you like that, but when I saw you living like this—" A quick gesture finished the sentence. Brittany looked around the room, seeing it through his eyes. She'd grown so accustomed to it that she'd almost forgotten how seedy it really was.

"It's the best I could manage." But the defensiveness had left her voice. She'd been trying to convince herself that she was managing okay, but he'd forced her to see that pride could only carry you so far. Still, she couldn't admit failure without a struggle.

"Do you have a better suggestion?" she asked, meeting his eyes challengingly.

"Yes, I do."

"Well, what is it?" she prodded when he didn't continue.

"You can marry me."

# Chapter Four

"What?" She'd never read anything that said that pregnancy caused auditory hallucinations, but that must be the case. It wasn't possible that he'd just said what she thought she'd heard.

"I want you to marry me."

There. She'd heard it again. If she was hearing things, would she have heard the same thing twice?

"You're kidding, right?"

"I'm not kidding," he said coolly, looking as if what he was suggesting wasn't the most incredible thing she could imagine.

"You have to be kidding," she told him a little desperately. She groped behind her for the dubious support of the stuffed chair. This was not a conversation to be had while standing.

"Why?"

"'Why?'" The simple question sent her thoughts stumbling. *Why* There were a thousand reasons, and she couldn't think of any of them.

"Why do I have to be kidding, Brittany? It's the

perfect solution.'' He sat on the edge of the sofa, leaning toward her.

"It's not perfect. It's insane."

"Why?"

"Would you stop asking that,'' she snapped. "It's perfectly obvious."

"Not to me. You need a place to stay. You need help with the baby. No matter how much pride you have, you've got to see that you can't stay here. Is this where you want to raise your child?"

"Of course not. This was only temporary."

"Until what? How are you going to get out of here?"

"I don't know,'' she admitted reluctantly. Hadn't she spent sleepless nights wondering just that?

"If you marry me, you'll have a place to stay. I've got a place outside Remembrance. It's not very big, but it's certainly better than this."

"Michael, you haven't thought this through. It doesn't make sense."

"Tell me what's wrong with the idea.'' His jaw set in a way that told her it wouldn't be easy to convince him of what should be obvious. And how did she go about convincing her foolish heart, which fairly leaped at the idea of having someone to share her burden? She tried to marshall her arguments, her fingers twisted together in her lap.

"I can't say that I'm not tempted,'' she began carefully. "I mean, it's pretty obvious that I'm not managing all that well on my own. I guess people with part of a degree in English aren't all that in demand."

She stopped but Michael said nothing. He only waited, as if confident that things were going to go precisely as he thought they should. Brittany felt a spurt of irritation at his confidence, but she was too tired for it to last long. She sighed.

"There's nothing in this for you, Michael. Maybe I've got an excess of pride, but I'd have to have none at all to accept what you're offering."

"I appreciate you looking out for my interests, Brittany, but I'm capable of doing it myself. And you're wrong. I would get something out of this marriage."

"What?"

"Peace of mind. I'd know that you were cared for. I wouldn't have to worry about you turning up in some worse dive than this."

"Why should you care so much?" she asked tiredly, leaning her head against the back of the chair. He hesitated, his eyes dropping to the tattered carpet.

"Dan was my closest friend, almost a brother to me. If the only thing I can do for him is take care of you, then I'd like to do it...if I can get some cooperation from you." He glanced at her, half smiling.

She didn't return the smile. She looked at him, her eyes searching. She wanted to say yes. She wanted to say yes to this whole insane proposal and know that she wasn't alone anymore.

"You can't base your whole life on doing what you think Dan would want."

"Not my whole life. Just until the baby is born and you've had a chance to get on your feet. What do they call it in all those romance novels? A marriage of convenience. It'll be temporary."

Brittany closed her eyes, shaking her head slowly against the temptation. How quickly all her determined independence faded when she was offered an alternative.

"No," she said at last, opening her eyes to look at

him. "There's just not enough in this for you. If you want to help me, I'm not so stupid that I won't let you, but you don't have to marry me."

"But marriage is the most practical way to go."

"Practical?" She laughed, feeling a touch of hysteria. "You're telling me this is practical?"

"Have you thought about what it's going to cost to have the baby?"

"Yes." She'd thought of little else the past few weeks.

"If you're my wife, my insurance will cover you and the child. Even once we're separated, the child will still be covered."

She wavered. He made it sound so reasonable, so logical. In her heart, she knew it was crazy, impractical, but oh, how she wanted to agree.

"I don't know," she muttered.

Michael reached out to catch her restless hands in his. "This is something I want to do, Brittany. Stop worrying about me and think about the baby. He'd have everything he needed, the best of care. You can't give him that if you're worried sick all the time."

"It might be a girl, you know."

"Then marry me and let me take care of you and *her*. You're not even eating right, now."

"I'm eating okay," she said fretfully, staring at their linked hands.

"Shall I go inventory your kitchen?"

"No." She sighed, knowing what he'd find. A jar of peanut butter, a box of saltines and a half a carton of milk weren't likely to convince him that she was following a nutritionally complete diet.

"Look, I'm not trying to make you feel like you've

failed. I just want you to see that you need some help.
There's nothing wrong with that.''

"I just don't see that you'd be getting much out of
this." But she was weakening. She could hear it in her
own voice, and she knew Michael could, too.

"Let me worry about that. Let me take care of you,
Brittany." She felt tears start to her eyes. Did he know
how much she wanted to say yes? She was so tired, so
awfully tired.

His hands felt strong on hers. His palms were rough
with calluses. Dan had told her once that Michael was
just as likely to work at framing a wall as he was at
designing the building it went in. They were good
hands, the kind of hands you could put your future into.

"I don't know," she whispered.

"I do." His fingers tightened over hers. "Come on,
Brittany. Say yes. This is my first marriage proposal.
You don't want to blight my life by turning me down,
do you?"

Her mouth trembled over a smile. He made it seem
so reasonable. He could even joke about it. Would it
really be so terrible of her to agree? As he said, it
would only be for a few months. And she had to think
of her child. Michael was right about the marriage offering some definite advantages to the child. Did she
have a right to put her pride over the welfare of her
baby?

"Are you sure about this? Really, really sure?"

"I'm really sure."

Her eyes searched his, looking for the doubts he had
to be feeling. But there was nothing but confidence to
be seen in those clear blue depths. It was a mad idea.

"It would only be for a few months," she said, more
to herself than to him.

"Just until you get on your feet," he promised.

"I can't believe I'm considering this!" She pulled her hands from his, standing up, needing to put some distance between them. It was too hard to think when he was sitting so close, making it all seem so plausible.

"It's a little unconventional, maybe, but it doesn't have to be forever."

She heard him stand up, but she didn't turn to look at him. Staring out the window, she tried to sort her thoughts. Twilight had fallen while they talked. She hadn't even noticed the fading light. Lights shone in the windows of the apartment building across the alley.

Darkness should have been kind to the shabby neighborhood, but it wasn't. The lack of light only seemed to emphasize the dinginess, the hopelessness that walked the streets.

Behind her, Michael snapped on a lamp. Brittany's fingers clenched on the windowsill as the light spilled out behind her. Maybe it was symbolic. She had to decide between the darkness she faced or the light Michael was holding out to her.

If it was wrong, she didn't want to know it. She was just too damned tired. She closed her eyes, leaning her forehead on the cool glass.

If Dan had still been alive... If Dan had been alive, none of this would be necessary. Things would have been the way she'd dreamed of them being. But Dan was dead and so were the dreams they'd shared.

She had to get on with her life as best as she could. Michael was offering her a way out.

"Brittany? Is it really so hard to decide?" His question held a note of uncertain humor. She turned away from the window, startled to find that he was standing right behind her. The light was behind him, leaving her in shadow.

"No. No, it's not so hard," she said softly. Drawing in a deep breath, she lifted her eyes to his, searching for some doubt. There was nothing there but confidence, something she dearly wished she had more of at this point. "Are you truly sure?"

"I'm truly sure," he told her gently. He reached out, tucking a stray lock of hair behind her ear. It took all Brittany's willpower not to close her eyes and lean into that touch. "Brittany, this is as much for me as it is for you. I *want* to do this."

He was so close his scent filled her nostrils, warm and male. How could he be so sure? She wanted to believe him—needed to. She was too tired to fight anymore.

"Yes." The word was barely a whisper, and Michael leaned closer, bending his head over hers.

"What?"

"I said yes. I'll marry you."

A quick intake of breath was the only sign of reaction for the space of several slow heartbeats. Brittany stared at the base of his throat, left bare by his open shirt. Why didn't he say something?

He touched her hair with gentle fingers, and she looked up at him, half-afraid of what she'd see. Was he regretting it already? His face was in shadow, making it difficult to read his expression, but she didn't think it was regret she saw there.

"Thank you."

"I think it should be the other way around. I should be thanking you," she said tiredly, finally giving in to the urge to lean her face against his hand. There was such strength in him. And she needed that strength right now. "I feel as if I'm using you. If it wasn't for the baby..."

"If it wasn't for the baby, the situation would be completely different," he agreed. "But that isn't the case. There's nothing wrong with taking help from a friend."

She laughed, barely holding back the sob that threatened to escape. "I think this is going a little above and beyond the call of friendship, but I can't argue anymore."

"How long will it take you to pack your things? I want you out of here tonight."

"Tonight?" She stepped away from him, looking around the shabby apartment. It wasn't that she'd been happy here, but it *had* been more or less home for the past weeks. "Where would I stay?"

"I'll take you to my parents. You can stay with them until I can make arrangements for us to be married. You don't *want* to stay here, do you?"

"Of course not. It's just that everything is happening so quickly. You can't show up on your parents' doorstep with me in tow. I mean, wouldn't you like a chance to prepare them?"

"I'm not leaving you alone here another night. Besides, my parents love surprises."


"Donovan, have you seen my gray blouse?" Beth's voice was muffled by the closet doors as she searched for the item in question.

Donovan stepped out of the bathroom, toweling his hair dry, another towel wrapped low on his hips. "Have I seen what?"

"My gray blouse. I can't find it."

"The one with the fancy buttons?"

"That's it. I was going to wear it tonight."

"Why don't you just wear what you have on?" He leaned one shoulder against the wall, admiring the view as Beth backed out of the closet. He couldn't put a name to what she was wearing, but he could describe them in one word. Sexy.

"Sure. That's a great idea. Go to the opening of a new restaurant wearing a camisole and tap pants."

"Is that what you call those things?"

"These *things* are pure silk and cost enough to balance the national debt."

"I guess I'll have to build another house to pay for them," he said lazily, reaching for her.

"Stop it." She leaned away from him, her hands on his chest, half laughing as he nuzzled the sensitive skin of her neck. "Donovan Sinclair, I want to go out tonight."

"I could make staying home an interesting proposition," he promised, his hand splayed across her upper back to hold her still for his exploring mouth.

"I'm sure you could," she said breathlessly. "But we promised Carol we'd be there."

"She'll be so busy she won't even notice whether we're there or not."

"You know she'll notice." Beth made the mistake of turning to look at him, and Donovan pounced, his lips catching hers. Beth melted, her arms stealing around his neck. The bedroom was silent for several long seconds. Beth gathered all her resources and wrenched her mouth from his, shoving at his shoulders until she could get enough room to breathe.

"Behave yourself," she ordered him.

"I thought you liked it when I misbehaved," he murmured, a wicked green light in his eyes.

"I mean it, Donovan."

"So do I."

"This is important to Carol. After all, she sold the nursery to buy this place. She really wants to make a success of it."

"Didn't I personally help her renovate it?" he asked in a injured tone, finally giving in and releasing her.

"Yes, you did a wonderful job, but this is her big opening night, and I think she needs our support."

"I think she's nuts," he grumbled, retreating into the bathroom to dispose of both towels. "The last thing this town needs is another restaurant."

"Carol thinks this one will be unique enough to attract business."

"With a name like El Gato Loco, the only thing it's going to attract is linguistics majors."

"I don't think it's that difficult to translate," Beth defended. "And I think The Crazy Cat is a great name for a restaurant with authentic Mexican food."

"I think she's going to lose her shirt." Donovan walked back into the bedroom, sans towel, and Beth felt her knees weaken.

He was so magnificently male. After all these years, just looking at him made her heart beat a little faster. He walked to the bed, reaching for his shorts before turning to see her watching him. Catching the look in her eyes, he grinned.

"Too late. You had your chance and you spurned me. Carol is expecting us."

"Well, we could be late."

"Certainly not. Wouldn't dream of it." His grin widened at the faint pout she affected. "We'll make up for it later."

"Promise?"

"Most definitely." He stepped into the shorts, and Beth returned her attention to the closet, finding the missing gray blouse hiding behind a rust-colored jacket. Shrugging into it, she moved over to the mirror, checking her makeup.

"Did Michael say whether or not he was coming tonight?"

"I didn't talk to him about it." Donovan's voice held a repressive note.

In the mirror, Beth could see him frown as he tucked his shirt into his slacks. "Problems?" she asked as she turned away from the mirror and picked up her skirt, a swingy affair of bright blue.

"I don't know. He was supposed to meet with some people at the Adams site today. He called, canceling at the last minute."

"He must have had a good reason."

"He said something about personal business."

"Well, it must have been important. That house is his pet project. He wouldn't have canceled on it for nothing."

"Well, I'd still like to know the reason. Adams called me, demanding an explanation."

Beth tugged the zipper up on her skirt. "It's been rough for Michael since Dan was killed."

"I know."

"And it didn't make it any easier that I lost the baby right before that. We weren't even here for him."

Donovan drew her into his arms, pressing his cheek to the golden softness of her hair. "It was bad timing all around, but I want you to stop acting like it was all your fault. The doctor said there was nothing anybody could have done to stop the miscarriage."

"I know." Her voice was muffled, and he knew she

was fighting back tears. In those first few weeks after the miscarriage, she'd never cried—not once. She'd held in all the grief and pain, growing pale and quiet, as if losing the baby had stolen a part of her soul. It wasn't until he'd taken her away, bullying her into going on the long cruise, that she'd finally begun to deal with the loss.

"But if I hadn't been such a dope about losing the baby, we would have been here when Michael got the news about Dan, instead of being out in the middle of the Pacific, where we couldn't do him any good."

"You weren't a dope. It was just one of those things. I don't know that we could have done much for him even if we had been here. It's been a long time since he came looking for us to get him through bad times."

"I still think it would have helped." She pushed back until she could meet his eyes. "He's been so quiet."

"Dan was his best friend. Michael will be okay. He just needs time."

"I guess." She sighed, her eyes still worried. "It's hard to remember that he's not a little boy anymore."

"He hasn't been a little boy for a very long time, love."

"I know." She shook her head, forcing a smile. "I'm just being silly."

"That's how I like you best." Donovan's eyes held a tender light that never failed to make her feel loved and protected. "Come on. If you're going to make me go to this shindig, let's get it over with."

He released her to walk across the room, and Beth felt a familiar twinge of regret at the limp that had forever replaced his old, powerful stride. It just didn't seem fair, but then it could have been much worse. So much worse, she reminded herself. She bent to slip on her shoes, remembering that rainy night, Michael's call from the hospital and later, much later, seeing the wreckage of that damned motorcycle and knowing how close she'd come to losing both husband and son.

"Beth? Are you coming?" Donovan turned at the door, arching one dark brow in question.

She crossed the room to him, linking her arm with his and leaning her head on his shoulder for an instant.

"I love you, Donovan Sinclair."

"I love you, too."

They were halfway down the stairs when they heard the sound of a key in the front door.

"Michael." Beth hurried down the stairs to greet her son. Donovan followed at a more leisurely pace, noting that Michael was not alone.

"Mom." Michael returned her hug, looking over her shoulder to meet his father's eyes. He released Beth, turning to draw Brittany forward. She'd hung back, her reluctance to be noticed obvious.

"You remember Brittany Winslow, don't you?"

"Of course." Beth held out her hand, her smile friendly. "You came to our Fourth of July party, didn't you?"

"Yes. I'm sorry to drop in on you like this, Mrs. Sinclair."

"Call me Beth, please."

"Thank you." Brittany's eyes dropped to the floor and stayed there. Donovan joined the group by the door, breaking the pause that threatened to stretch to awkward lengths.

"Hello, Michael. Brittany, nice to see you again."

"I'm sorry we've sort of popped in like this, but I'd like to talk to you, if you've got a few minutes."

"Of course." Beth hadn't been a mother all these years without learning to recognize the strain in her son's voice.

"It looks like you were going out," Michael said.

"Nothing that can't be postponed," Donovan said. "Why don't we go into the living room and sit down?"

Michael took Brittany's arm, feeling her tension as he led her into the living room. She'd argued all the way here that he couldn't just drop her *and* the news that they were getting married on his parents all at once. And he'd told her over and over again that there was nothing to worry about.

Now that he was here, he wasn't quite so sure. It *was* an awful lot to absorb. On the other hand, he didn't really have a choice. If he and Brittany were to be married as soon as possible, then he could hardly delay letting his family know about it.

Brittany sat on the edge of a chair, her feet precisely together, her hands clasped in her lap. She looked as though she were on the way to her own execution. Michael chose to sit on the arm of her chair, half-afraid that if he didn't stay close, she might bolt for the door.

Beth settled onto the sofa, and Donovan chose a stance near the fireplace, leaning one arm on the mantel. Once they were all comfortable, no one said anything for the space of several seconds. Donovan's eyes seemed watchful, Beth's curious.

"What did you want to talk to us about?" Donovan finally asked.

Michael felt Brittany start. He cleared his throat. "Actually, I've got a bit of a surprise for you both." *Wrong tone, idiot. Don't sound so jovial. You sound like Ed McMahon about to announce a new winner in a sweepstakes.*

"A surprise?" Beth's smile was intact, but the look she gave Donovan was uneasy.

"Brittany and I are getting married. Immediately."

The words came out stark and unadorned. They seemed to lie in the air as if painted in flaming red. No one said a word. Donovan didn't move, didn't by so much as a flicker of an eyebrow reveal his reaction to the news. Beth opened her mouth, closed it, opened it again, then she sat back on the sofa without speaking, her wide blue eyes fixed on her son.

Brittany, glancing down at the floor, looked as though she were going to faint. There wasn't a trace of color to be seen in her face, and her fingers were knotted together in her lap. He felt a surge of protectiveness, a feeling that was rapidly becoming familiar.

He dropped his hand to her shoulder, telling her silently that everything was going to be okay. His eyes took on a faint challenge when he looked at his parents.

"I realize this must be a surprise to you."

"Well, yes, it is rather." Beth glanced at Donovan as if trying to read something in his expression. He returned her look with an arched brow.

"Don't look at me. I had no idea."

"No one did. We just decided this afternoon. I was hoping Brittany could stay with you until I can arrange for us to be married."

"I... Well, we..." Beth trailed off, staring at him helplessly.

"What your mother is trying to say is that we're both still a little dazed by this news. We didn't even know the two of you were seeing each other."

Brittany reached up, clutching at Michael's hand. He returned the pressure with a reassuring squeeze.

"Like I said, it's been a little sudden for us, too."

"Are you sure this is what you want to do?" Beth asked worriedly.

"We're certain."

"But why rush things? Why not take your time to plan a wonderful wedding?"

"We've got a good reason for rushing things," Michael replied. Brittany's fingers tightened over his, a silent plea in the gesture. But his parents were going to have to know. "Brittany is pregnant, Mom."

"Pregnant? But I thought you and Dan—" Beth broke off, color flooding into her face. "I'm sorry. I didn't mean to... I just..." She trailed off weakly.

Michael drew Brittany closer, the possessiveness of the gesture clear. "I'm very excited about the baby," he said firmly.

"No one said you shouldn't be, Michael." That was Donovan, his voice calm, though his eyes reflected his shock. He came forward, placing his hand on Beth's shoulder. "We just weren't expecting—"

"No." Brittany's protest cut into words. It was the first thing she'd said since the conversation began. She straightened away from Michael's supporting arm, drawing in a deep breath. There was not a trace of color in her face, but her chin was set with determination.

"Brittany—"

"No, Michael. I want them to know the truth."

"I think we'd all like that," Donovan agreed.

"This isn't Michael's baby. It's Dan's. Michael told me that I didn't have to tell you the truth, but I think you should know."

"Thank you," Beth said weakly. She reached up to catch Donovan's hand, clinging to it as if to a lifeline.

"I'm sure you can see why we want to get married right away." Michael's eyes held a cool challenge.

"Well, actually..." Beth began, but Donovan squeezed her hand, cutting off her protest.

"Look, I hate to sound terribly old-world and chauvinistic, but do you think I could talk to Michael alone, Beth?"

She looked up at him, reading the plea in his eyes. Every instinct cried out that she had to talk to her son, had to try to understand what was going on here. But maybe Donovan was right. The two of them had always been close. Maybe this was something better worked out between them.

"All right." She drew a deep breath and stood up, forcing a smile as she looked at Brittany. "Would you like a cup of tea?"

Brittany hesitated, glancing up at Michael before nodding. "Thank you."

Michael rose as Brittany stood up, watching her leave the room with his mother.

"Your mother isn't going to put arsenic in her tea," Donovan said drily.

"I know. It's just that Brittany is rather fragile at the moment."

"Aren't we all," Donovan muttered. "You want to tell me the full story?"

Michael shrugged. "There's not really all that much to tell. Brittany needs someone to take care of her until the baby is born."

"I can appreciate that. But marriage? Can't you help her without marrying her?"

"This is the best way. She and the baby will qualify for my insurance coverage. She'll have a place to stay, someone to look out for her."

"What about you?" Donovan asked quietly. "What is this going to mean to you?"

Michael took his time with the answer, trying to find the words to explain something he didn't entirely understand.

"Dan was my best friend. He loved Brittany and I think he would have married her had he known the circumstances. It sounds corny, but I feel as I owe him this much by stepping in."

"It's not going to be easy. Marriage is tough enough, but when you add a baby into it…" Donovan shook his head, remembering the early days with Beth, the strain, the pressure.

"I don't expect it to be a walk in the park. But you and Mom managed it. I don't see why Brittany and I can't do the same."

"Your mother and I loved each other. Can you say the same?"

"Do you use sugar?"

"Yes, thank you." The short exchange was the first thing either of them had said since leaving Michael and Donovan.

Brittany watched as Beth moved around the kitchen, preparing tea. The other woman's movements were stiff, reflecting her distraction. Tea was the last thing on either of their minds. Beth set a cup of steaming liquid in front of her. Brittany lifted the sugar spoon, but her fingers were trembling so much she ended up with at least as much sugar on the table as in her cup.

"I'm sorry." She dabbed at the spilled sugar, fighting the burning sensation in her eyes.

"It's all right." Staring at the girl's downcast head, Beth felt a wave of sympathy. She'd been younger than Brittany when Michael was conceived, but the experience of finding yourself with an unplanned pregnancy couldn't be easy at any age. "I won't bite, you know."

"I know." Brittany's voice shook, and she refused to lift her head. "You must think I'm the most awful person."

"I don't think you're awful at all. I am worried," she said carefully. "Marriage seems..." She waved her hand, lacking the words to explain what she was thinking.

"It was Michael's idea. In fact, he insisted. I suppose I should have been stronger." She stared at her teacup. Beth waited, sensing there was more to come. Brittany looked up suddenly, her eyes catching Beth's.

"I've been so frightened. After Dan died, I was alone. Michael is so strong and I...I need that strength. I know I shouldn't let him do this, but I..." She stopped, her eyes dropping away. Her voice shook when she went on. "Have you ever been all alone and so scared you could hardly breathe sometimes? If it was just me, I'd have been all right. But there's the baby."

"What about your parents?" Beth asked softly. Despite herself, she was moved by Brittany's pain. "Couldn't they help you?"

"My parents." Brittany laughed, a short, harsh sound. "When I told my parents about the baby, they wanted to send me off somewhere to have it and then give it away. They were worried about what the neighbors might think if their daughter had a child out of wedlock."

"Your poor thing." Beth remembered how frightened she'd been when she told her father she was pregnant. Looking back, she could see that he must have been angry and scared for her, but there'd never been so much as an instant when he'd made her feel less than loved, less than wanted. What must it be like to have your own family turn their backs on you? "It must have been just awful for you."

Brittany blinked back tears. The concern in Beth's voice was everything she hadn't gotten from her own mother.

"I know you must think I'm awful to let Michael do this for me. But it's only until the baby is here."

"You make it sound so simple, Brittany. A marriage, for any reason, is very complex." Beth shook her head, maternal concern warring with compassion for the girl across the table.

"You don't get married and simply remain two people living together. There's you and your husband, and then there's this third entity that's the marriage. It takes on a life of its own. You've got a whole new set of loyalties, new ties, new demands."

"I know it might not be as easy as it seems now," Brittany said slowly. "But I think if we're careful, we can make it work. Michael seems to feel that he needs to do this for Dan's sake, and I don't want to struggle on my own anymore. I want—need—what he wants to give. I won't hurt him. I promise you that. I won't hurt him, no matter what."

Beth looked at her, seeing the sincerity in those big gray eyes, the fragility in the delicate bone structure. She was so young. When you were young it was easy to make promises about not hurting someone. And you believed them. Life had a way of interfering with promises like that.

She sighed, feeling suddenly very old. "I won't fight you on this, Brittany. I honestly don't know if you're doing the right thing or not. But I know Michael well enough to know that he's made up his mind, and I'll just have to trust his judgment.''

"Thank you. Beth.'' The name came as an awkward afterthought. She smiled, a hesitant expression that lighted her pale face with genuine beauty. Beth looked at her, wondering how it was possible that Michael wouldn't get hurt.

# Chapter Five

The wedding was held in Donovan and Beth's home. Besides the bride and groom and justice of the peace, the only guests were Beth and Donovan and Brittany's friend Janie. Brittany didn't throw her tiny bouquet of white roses and baby's breath, nor did anyone toss rice at the newlyweds.

Brittany listened to the solemn words of the ceremony, her head bent, her eyes focused on nothing in particular. This wasn't the way it was supposed to be. This wasn't the way she'd dreamed of her wedding. There should have been laughter and lots of guests, and she should have been wildly happy.

And Dan should have been standing beside her.

She stared at her fingers lying in Michael's. His hand was so much larger than hers. There was strength there. And compassion.

"Do you, Michael Patrick Sinclair, take this woman to be your lawfully wedded wife? To have and to hold, to love and to cherish from this day forward as long as you both shall live?"

"I do."

How could he sound so confident, so calm? It was all a lie. They weren't going to love and cherish or have and hold. Those words were meant for other couples, couples who were in love, who were marrying for the right reasons.

"Brittany?" The minister's quiet voice broke into her circling thoughts, calling her back to the matters at hand. She realized it must be time for her response. She couldn't do it. She just couldn't promise those things.

Michael's hand tightened over hers, and she looked up, meeting his eyes. She could lose herself in those eyes, clear blue and as deep as the ocean. His eyes promised her that everything was going to be all right. He'd make sure of it. She looked into his eyes and clung to his hand.

"I do." The response was hardly a whisper, but it was enough.

She didn't hear the rest of the ceremony, was barely aware of the minister pronouncing them man and wife. She never took her eyes off Michael's, feeling as if they were the only lifeline she had. Michael's head lowered, his hand gently squeezing hers. This must be the part where he was supposed to kiss the bride.

She felt a momentary panic, as if, in some way, having him kiss her were more frightening than the ceremony itself. His free hand came up, his palm slightly rough against the softness of her cheek. She closed her eyes as his mouth touched hers. It was a gentle kiss, given without demands. His mouth was warm against hers, and she found herself relaxing, returning the kiss in the same spirit.

Her lashes came up as he lifted his head. There was

something in his eyes she couldn't quite read. A question? A need? The expression was gone so quickly, she half thought she'd imagined it.

"Congratulations." Beth was the first to come forward, her smile contrasting with the worry in her eyes. Brittany returned her hug, grateful for the show of support. In the few days since Michael had brought her here, she'd found his parents to be warm and supportive.

They might not agree that marriage was the best thing but, having accepted the reality of it, they'd gone out of their way to make Brittany feel comfortable.

It had been Beth who had insisted that Brittany have a wedding gown. And Beth who'd taken her shopping, helping her choose the simple ivory dress she now wore.

"Welcome to the family," Donovan said, and Brittany lifted her cheek to accept his kiss. Donovan wasn't as easy to know as Beth. There was a reserve about him that reminded her of Michael. But there was an underlying warmth, too.

"Congratulations, Brittany." Janie's words were a little hesitant, as if she wasn't quite sure whether or not congratulations were in order.

"Thank you." Brittany glanced at her friend, then she returned her gaze to the small bouquet she held. Donovan had handed her the bouquet just before the ceremony, his smile kind, as if he'd sensed the panic she was feeling. She smoothed a rose petal with one shaking finger, thinking of her own parents.

"Well, I think we should have some champagne to celebrate," Beth said, her tone hearty.

Despite the effort everyone put forth, the mood could not have been called exactly jovial. Odd little silences were prone to fall and then be broken just as suddenly. Beth sat very close to Donovan, as if needing the support of his nearness.

Brittany said very little. She couldn't seem to get words out past the tightness in her throat. None of this felt real. She felt like an actress in a play, only she couldn't quite remember her lines.

Janie left as soon as was polite. Brittany saw her to the door.

"You keep in touch," Janie told her, giving her a rather fierce hug.

"Of course I will." Brittany returned the hug, feeling a tiny crack in the wall that separated her from the rest of the world.

"I think your Michael is terrific. Give him a chance, Britt."

She was gone before Brittany could say anything, hurrying down the steps. Brittany watched her go, her fingers tight around the edge of the door. She was oblivious to the cool evening air as she watched the taillights of Janie's little compact disappear. She felt as if she were seeing the last trace of her old life vanish— the life she understood.

Stupid. That life had ended when the child she was carrying was conceived. And Dan's death had made her realize she couldn't go back. Not ever.

Her Michael? He wasn't *her* Michael. Or at least, if he was, it was only temporary. As if he were on loan. Like a library book. She giggled at the thought. The hysteria underlying the sound startled her, and feeling self-conscious, she put a hand over her mouth.

"Brittany?" She jumped at the sound of Michael's voice. "Are you okay?"

"I'm fine." She shut the door carefully before turning to look at him. "Just a little tired, I guess."

"We can go home now, if you'd like."

She pushed back a tendril of hair that had fallen loose from her chignon, suddenly aware of how tired she really was. It had been so long since she'd been able to rest without some worry nagging at her—since she'd realized she was pregnant.

"I'd like that, if your parents wouldn't think it was too rude."

Michael gave her a crooked smile. "I don't think this has been any easier on them than it has on us. They'll probably be glad to see us go."

Michael's house was on the outskirts of Remembrance, backed by rolling fields. It was land he'd bought from his father. He'd built the house himself, much of it with his own hands.

Approaching it in the darkness, Brittany could make out only the shape of it. A high peaked roof outlined against the night sky, wide windows that reflected the headlights as they pulled into the driveway. Michael shut off the engine, and silence suddenly became a third presence.

He didn't say anything or seem to expect her to. He thrust open his door, coming around to open hers while she was still staring at the house. Brittany took the hand he held out to her, feeling, as always, the strength of him. This time, it sent a shiver up her spine. Staring up at him in the darkness, she could make out nothing beyond the shape of him—tall, broad shouldered.

Why hadn't she ever noticed how big he was? Maybe even an inch or two taller than Dan's six foot. He seemed to tower over her in the darkness.

What had she done? She barely knew this man. Oh, she knew he'd been Dan's friend, the quiet one of the duo. And she knew he'd been kind to her. But she didn't really *know* him.

And she'd just married him.

She shivered and Michael felt it through the hand he still held. Mistaking the reason, he drew her closer.

"I guess autumn is really here. It's chilly after the sun goes down. Let's get you in the house. I can get your suitcase later."

Brittany let him lead her toward the house simply because there was nowhere else to go. She was overwhelmingly aware that she'd just made a major commitment to this man—a near stranger.

Michael unlocked the door, flipping on a light as they stepped through.

"The living room is through here."

Brittany went in the direction he pointed, stepping onto thick carpeting. A huge stone fireplace dominated one wall; the rest of the room was almost stark in its simplicity. It was a man's room—heavy leather furniture designed for comfort, a few paintings and none of the quirky little touches a woman might have added. Brittany felt like an alien presence.

"It's pretty austere, I suppose." She turned to see Michael frowning as he looked around the room, as if trying to see it through her eyes.

"Oh no. It's beautiful, really."

He shrugged. "I furnished it for comfort, not style. You're welcome to make changes if you want."

"Oh no. I wouldn't dream of fiddling with your home."

"Brittany, it's your home now. Even if it's only for

a while. I want you to be comfortable here. Besides, the place could probably use a little sprucing up."

"Home," she repeated, looking around the big room. Home. It didn't feel like home. But then, she couldn't imagine what would right now.

"I didn't know you played guitar."

Michael followed her gaze to the guitar that sat propped in a corner. "I don't. At least not very well. It's something I like to relax with once in a while. You can let me know if it bothers you."

He crossed to the fireplace, kneeling to set a match to the wood pile that already lay there. Flames devoured the crumpled newspapers and licked up through the stack of kindling before reaching the small logs.

"It's a little early in the year for a fire, but I like the look of it." He stood up, dusting his hands together as he stared down into the small blaze.

"I guess it's just now occurring to me what a disruption this is going to cause in your life," Brittany said slowly.

He turned, arching a brow when he saw that she was still standing in the middle of the floor. "There isn't a whole lot to disrupt, believe me. Have a seat. You look like you're getting ready to leave. You want something to drink or eat? You didn't eat much at supper."

Brittany sank onto the sofa, her eyes skimming the room again, trying to develop a picture of the man she'd married a few hours before. She'd given so much thought to what this marriage was going to mean to her and so little to what it was going to mean to him.

"You know, I never even asked if you had a girlfriend who might object to this arrangement."

"I don't."

"But I should have asked," she insisted. "I've only

been thinking about how this is going to affect my life. I've given hardly a thought to what it's going to do to yours."

"I told you before, I'm perfectly capable of looking out for my own interests. You don't have to worry about me, Brittany."

"But I should have thought about it." Her eyes reflected her distress. Michael came and sat on the huge glass-topped coffee table in front of her. In the dim light cast by the fire, his eyes appeared midnight blue.

"I don't want you to worry about anything but yourself and the baby. The whole purpose of this is to make sure that the two of you are okay."

Her eyes dropped to where her fingers were restlessly pleating the ivory silk of her dress. "I can't just not think about it. You're doing so much for me."

"I told you before that this is something I *want* to do." He reached out, catching her hand in his. "I want to do this for Dan."

It was the first time either of them had mentioned Dan's name in days. Reminded of her loss, Brittany felt the familiar wave of grief wash over her. But it was gentler now, more a deep sadness than raging pain. Without realizing it, she was coming to terms with the loss.

Perhaps Michael felt the same rush of pain. His fingers tightened over hers for an instant. The only sound in the room was the crackle of the fire. Outside, an owl called mournfully as if seeking something forever lost. Michael drew a deep breath, forcing a light note into his voice.

"Besides, you make it sound like I've sentenced myself to hard labor. I can think of worse fates than to be married to a beautiful woman. I'll be the envy of all my friends.''

Brittany withdrew her hand from his, reaching up to tuck a loose strand of hair back. Her smile might be a little wavery around the edges, but she was determined to follow his lead.

"In a few months I'm going to look like a water buffalo. I don't think your friends are going to be terribly envious then.''

"Sure they will. None of them have a water buffalo in the house.''

She glanced up, catching the teasing light in his eyes. Her mouth curved up in the first genuine humor she'd felt in weeks. The movement felt rusty.

"Thanks. Just wait till you have to install a hoist to get me out of the tub, and then see how you feel.''

"I'm sure I'll cope.'' He stood up abruptly. "I'm going to make some cocoa.''

"Cocoa?''

"Sure. The perfect thing to sip by the fire. Besides, aren't pregnant women supposed to drink lots of milk?''

He was on his way out of the room as he spoke, apparently feeling that a reply wasn't essential. Brittany looked after him, wondering if she'd said something to upset him.

In the kitchen, Michael pulled open the refrigerator door with such force that a bottle of salad dressing tumbled out, cracking on the tile. Muttering a curse, he took out the milk, pouring it into a pan and setting it on the stove before grabbing a towel to mop up the mess on the floor.

This wasn't going to be as easy as he'd thought it would be. He'd had it all planned. They'd live together, but it would be more in the nature of a platonic friendship than husband and wife. He'd make sure that she got the care she needed—the only thing he could do for Dan.

In a year or so their lives would go in different directions. Sure, there'd still be ties, but this would just become a rather peculiar interlude in both their lives.

It had only taken Brittany's joking words to tell him that it wasn't going to be as easy as he'd tried to believe. The thought of her in the bath created vivid and unwelcome images in his mind. Her skin would be moist, little drops of water pearling on her shoulders and breasts.

It would be a bubble bath in which the fluffy white foam would float over the surface of the water, offering tantalizing glimpses of creamy skin. She'd have her hair up in one of those casually twisted knots on top of her head, but several tendrils would be loose, caressing the nape of her neck.

She'd look up at him, those wide gray eyes all soft and wanting. And her mouth—her lower lip would be just slightly thrust out in anticipation of his kiss. He'd kneel beside the tub and—

A stab of pain slashed through the image. With a curse, he dropped the piece of glass, staring at the blood welling up at the base of his thumb. Standing up and moving to the sink he thrust his hand under a stream of cold water. What he really needed was a cold shower.

What was happening? He had no business conjuring erotic fantasies about Brittany. She was Dan's girl.

*And your wife.*

But that was just an arrangement to take care of her. It was temporary.

*But you never discussed the sleeping arrangements with her.*

They didn't need to be discussed. He'd already cleared out a bedroom for her. He shook his head, wishing he could clear out his mind as easily.

The wedding today hadn't been quite what he'd expected. When they'd decided to get married, he'd looked on it as a necessary step. He hadn't given any thought to the actual marriage. Although, if he had thought about it, he wouldn't have expected the ceremony to have any effect on him. It was just a minor detail—something that had to be done before they could go on to more important things.

Then he'd seen Brittany in her wedding dress. It wasn't a real wedding dress, with yards of lace and ten feet of train. There'd been no veil, no ruffles. Just plain ivory silk, high at the neck and long sleeved, with a full skirt that fell to past her knees.

When he thought about it, there was nothing spectacular about the dress. Yet, in the first moment that he'd seen her coming down the stairs, she'd taken his breath away.

During the ceremony, he'd found his eyes drawn to her. The words the minister was saying, words he'd more or less expected to ignore, had suddenly seemed full of meaning. To love and cherish, to have and to hold. They were just words, but he couldn't deny that he'd felt guilty at taking the vows, knowing that there was no truth in them.

Angry hissing made him jerk his hand out of the water and turn toward the stove. Milk foamed over the top of the pan, bubbling onto the stove top with evil pleasure, there to burn to brown crust. Michael's hand was numb from having rested under the cold water so long, but it wasn't so numb that he couldn't feel the pain when he unthinkingly grabbed the pan's handle with his bare hand.

He yelped, jerking back, upsetting the pan, thus creating the final disaster as it tipped, spilling scalding milk down the front of the stove. Nursing his wounded hand, he stared at the mess. This was his punishment for having lascivious thoughts about a woman he had no business having such thoughts about.

"Wages of sin," he mumbled, thrusting his uninjured hand through his hair. By now, Brittany was probably wondering if he'd had to milk a cow to get the milk for cocoa.

When Michael stepped into the living room, prepared to tell her that the only way she was going to get cocoa was if she wanted to go to the all-night café a few miles down the road, he saw that explanations weren't necessary.

The fire still burned, sending tongues of flame up the chimney, but Brittany wasn't watching it. She'd kicked off her shoes, curling her legs under her. Her head was propped rather awkwardly against the arm of the couch, and she was sound asleep.

Looking at her, Michael felt a wave of emotion he couldn't quite define. She looked so small and vulnerable. He wanted to protect her, keep her safe.

"A lousy protector you'd make," he muttered jeeringly. "You just about killed yourself in your own kitchen."

But the feeling persisted, irritating him. He reached out to shake her awake but drew back without touching her. She looked so tired. The past few months seemed to have drained all the energy from her.

Mumbling at his own stupidity, he bent and scooped

her up into his arms. She stirred as if waking and then
settled more comfortably against him, turning her face
into his neck. Her weight seemed insubstantial as he
carried her into the bedroom. She was going to have
to start eating more. He didn't know much about pregnant women, but he was willing to bet that Brittany
hadn't been eating the way she should.

Michael sat her on the bed and then straightened up.
Looking at her, he hesitated. She wasn't going to be
very comfortable the way she was.

"Brittany?" He called her name quietly, giving one
shoulder a gentle nudge. She mumbled in her sleep but
didn't wake. "Brittany?" He tried again but it was
clear it was going to take more than that to wake her.
Even when he clicked on the bedside lamp, she didn't
twitch. In this light, the smudgy purple shadows under
her eyes were easy to see.

With a sigh, he turned her until he could see the row
of buttons at the back of her dress. Manipulating the
tiny globes through loops that seemed one size too
small, he tried not to think about what he was doing.
He didn't need to remember that it was his wife he was
undressing or that this was their wedding night or just
how beautiful she looked when she smiled.

Unbuttoned, the dress was not difficult to ease off,
leaving her clad in a pale slip and panty hose. Michael
hesitated only a moment before deciding not to push
his luck. The hose could stay precisely where they
were. Rolling Brittany to one side, he pulled back the
covers before lifting to lay her against the sheets.

She stirred as the cool cotton touched her bare shoulders, her mouth curving in a smile of sensual sweet-
ness. Her eyes still closed, her hand lifted, seeking.

Michael caught it, feeling the fragility of her fingers against his.

"Mmm?" This time her murmur held a questioning note, and her lashes stirred as if she were trying to wake.

"Go back to sleep." He brushed her hair back from her forehead with his free hand, wondering at the softness of the tendrils that clung to his fingers. "Go to sleep," he whispered.

The sound of his voice seemed to relax her. As she sank deeper into the pillow, her mouth remained tilted up at the corners. She sighed.

"Dan."

Michael's fingers froze against her forehead. For a slow count of five, he didn't move. Then he slowly lowered her hand, tucking it carefully under the covers. His face was without expression as he reached out to snap off the lamp and left the room, shutting the door behind him.

The fire still flickered in the living room, though it was burning low. Crossing the room to a shallow cupboard built against one wall, he took out a bottle of whiskey and poured a shot into a small glass, then without hesitation, knocked it back neat. It burned in his throat before settling in a warm lump in his gut. He poured another shot before capping the bottle and putting it away.

Carrying the glass over to the fire, he stumbled over one of Brittany's shoes. Sinking into a chair, he reached down to pick it up. Such a tiny foot.

*Dan.*

He took a swallow of whiskey. *Whose name did you expect her to say, dope? Yours? Not bloody likely.* Besides, he didn't want her muttering his name in her sleep, anyway. This whole arrangement was temporary. It would soon be over. It wouldn't do to forget that.

It also wouldn't do to forget that the only reason Brittany had agreed to marry him was because the alternative was even worse than the solution. As soon as she'd had the baby and gotten on her feet, she was going to be out of the marriage as fast as you could say divorce. Or annulment. Hell, he didn't even know which it would be.

He took another swallow of whiskey, frowning at the shoe in his hand. Right now, she needed him. When she didn't need him anymore, she'd be gone. Which was exactly the way he wanted it.

He tossed back the last of the whiskey, then he set the glass down with a thump. Everything was going to work out just the way he'd planned it. He'd help Brittany for Dan's sake, a last favor for a friend. That's all there was to it.

*Dan.*

The shoe hit the far wall with a satisfying thump before bouncing back onto the carpeting. Michael glared at it, wishing he had another whiskey.

The first thing Brittany was aware of was feeling rested, something she hadn't felt in a long time. She kept her eyes closed, snuggling deeper into the pillow. The bed had never felt better. She wanted nothing more than to lie just where she was, eyes closed, the rest of the world a distant annoyance.

But once awake, there was no coaxing sleep back. With a frown, she buried her face in the pillow. Memories were intruding on the sleepy content she was trying to cling to. The bed, though comfortable, was unfamiliar. The light came from the wrong direction.

Michael. With a groan, she turned over, opening her eyes. She'd gotten married yesterday. She was in Michael's house—her husband's house. The ceiling was open-beamed pine, giving the room a feeling at once rustic and airy. The furniture was also pine. The overall motif was country without being cutesy.

Pulling herself upright against the pillows, she pushed her hair back from her face, trying to piece together how she'd gotten here. The last thing she remembered was Michael going off to make cocoa. She'd been staring into the fireplace, too tired to even worry about the huge step she'd taken. That was the last thing she could remember. She must have fallen asleep on the sofa, and Michael had brought her in here.

Spotting her dress draped over the back of a chair, she realized that that wasn't all he'd done. She pushed back the covers, relieved to find that he'd stopped with the dress. The thought of Michael undressing her was disturbing. It seemed so intimate. She shook her head. Her full slip was more modest than a lot of things women wore on the street.

Sitting up straighter, she swung her legs over the side of the bed, waiting for the vague queasiness to subside before she tried to stand up. She'd been lucky so far. Morning sickness hadn't been a problem. Hopefully, it would stay that way.

There was a bathroom connected to the bedroom, where Brittany took time to wash her face and comb her hair before venturing back into the bedroom in search of clothes. There was no sign of the suitcase she'd brought from Beth and Donovan's after the wedding, but the boxes in the corner held the rest of her things. Michael had brought them over two days ago.

It didn't take long to slip into a pair of jeans and a

shirt. She wore the shirt out, letting the long tails hide the fact that she couldn't snap her jeans anymore. She was going to have to buy some new clothes. She frowned as she finished buttoning the shirt. Finances were another thing she and Michael hadn't discussed in detail.

In fact, it was only now—after they were married—that she was realizing just how few things they *had* discussed. Brittany frowned at her refelction in the mirror as she pinned her hair back off her face. Maybe accepting the idea that she was going to marry him was all she'd been able to deal with at first. Now that that was a reality, she was starting to wonder about the details of this arrangement.

The first thing to do was to get up the courage to leave the sanctuary of the bedroom and face Michael. Her husband. Michael was her husband. She was his wife. No matter how she phrased it, she couldn't make it seem real. The ceremony the day before was already vague, dreamlike, as if it were part of someone else's life.

Only it wasn't. She, Brittany Winslow, was now Brittany Sinclair, and she might as well get used to the idea. Drawing a deep breath, she opened the door and stepped into the hallway.

Sunlight spilled through a bank of high, narrow windows along one wall, making the hallway much brighter than might have been expected. There was a door at the far end that she assumed must lead to Michael's bedroom. From the stillness of the house, it appeared that he was still sleeping.

As it turned out, he was asleep but not in his bedroom. Brittany was halfway across the living room before she realized that she wasn't alone. Michael was sprawled in the wide leather chair in front of the fireplace, his long legs draped awkwardly over the arm, his neck at an impossible angle.

Her first urge was to retreat to the bedroom, which already seemed a haven. She squelched it immediately. She couldn't run every time she saw Michael. Besides, he didn't even know she was here. Despite herself, she was drawn closer, studying his sleeping face.

He looked younger. Sleep eased the maturity from his face, leaving him vulnerable. Odd, she'd never really noticed just how handsome he was. She'd always been vaguely aware that he was attractive, but all her attention had been for Dan.

If she'd been asked, she'd have said that Dan's sandy-brown hair and light blue eyes were surely the epitome of male beauty. Yet, there was something appealing in Michael's darker good looks.

A lock of tobacco-brown hair had fallen across his forehead, and she reached out to push it back, surprised by the silky feel of it against her fingers. She drew her hand back, oddly disturbed. She wasn't sure she wanted to see him like this—soft, vulnerable, more human, somehow.

She'd had this vague idea that, even after they were married, they'd remain somewhat distant from each other. She hadn't thought about what it was going to be like to live with him, to see him across the breakfast table, to bump into him after a shower, to see him vulnerable as he was now.

Brittany turned away, uncomfortable without being able to put a precise name to what it was that bothered her. She was just imagining things. Weren't pregnant women supposed to be prone to flights of fancy? So she'd seen Michael asleep. So what?

All it took was seeing the kitchen to bring her solidly to earth again. It was basically a rather nice kitchen. Compact but designed so that it looked bigger than it actually was. It wasn't the decor that brought her to a halt.

On the floor in front of the refrigerator was a puddle of blue cheese dressing, a broken bottle floating forlornly in the middle. On the counter were two cups and a box of cocoa. On the stove was a pan, and all over the stove was what must have been the contents of the pan.

She was on her knees mopping up the dressing when a small sound made her glance up. Once Michael came around the corner, he stopped dead, obviously surprised to see her.

"Brittany." He thrust his fingers through his hair, rumpling it into soft brown waves. "I thought you'd still be asleep."

"I've been up a few minutes." She returned her attention to the dressing, picking pieces of broken glass out of the mess and dropping them into the dustpan she'd found behind the door.

"Here, you don't have to do that. I should have cleaned it up last night." He crouched beside her, reaching for the dustpan, but she moved it out of reach.

"I'll do it."

"I'm the one who broke the bottle."

"And let the milk boil over." She looked up in time to see his guilty glance at the stove.

"Things didn't go so well last night. It's just as well you fell asleep. But I didn't leave the mess for you to clean up. I was going to do it myself."

"But you fell asleep."

"Well, I'm awake now and I can take care of it."

Brittany reached for a roll of paper towels and started to sop up the sticky dressing, ignoring Michael's halfhearted attempt to take paper towels away from her.

"You know, I was actually rather relieved to see the kitchen like this."

"Relieved?" He said, looking surprised. "You like filthy kitchens?"

"Not particularly." She threw the wet towels into the trash can and sat back on her heels, looking at him. "But it was nice to find out that you aren't entirely perfect."

Surprise flared in his eyes. "You must be thinking of someone else," he said at last. "'Perfect' is not a word even my own mother would apply to me."

"Well, these past few days, you've been so calm. In complete control. It can be a little intimidating."

He reached out to catch her hand when she moved to stand up. "Do I intimidate you?"

Brittany stared at their linked hands. The plain gold wedding band on her third finger caught the sunlight pouring in through the window over the sink.

"Not 'intimidate,' precisely," she said quietly.

"What 'precisely'?" he pressed.

"You seem to know exactly where you're going and exactly what you want. I feel like I've been floundering for the past couple of months. Since…since Dan's plane went down, I haven't been able to focus on much of anything."

"I think that's understandable." His thumb rubbed the wedding ring. "You've had a lot to wade through."

"I suppose." She sighed, looking up at him. "Why do I have the feeling that, if you were in my shoes, you would have managed better than I did?"

"If I were in your shoes, I'd have been in every medical journal in the country."

He said it so seriously that it took a minute for his meaning to sink in. When it did, she felt a smile crack, and then laughter welled up. The sound was rusty but it was definitely a laugh. It felt wonderful. As if she'd been only half-alive for a long time. Now life was pouring back into her veins.

Kneeling there on the kitchen floor, her hand still in Michael's, their shared laughter mingling in the morning air, Brittany felt a surge of optimism. Life *did* go on. Maybe it could even be good again.

## Chapter Six

The next few weeks were full of adjustments. Adjusting to marriage, adjusting to each other and, for Brittany, adjusting to all the changes in her body. The past was pushed into the background by the necessity of figuring out the present.

Brittany still wore the locket Dan had given her, but she thought about him less often. There was so much to deal with in her life right now that she didn't have time to think about her loss. When she did think about it, she found the pain growing less acute.

Michael did everything he could to make her life comfortable. He bought her a car, used but reliable, so that she wouldn't have to rely on him for transportation. When she protested that he was spending too much money on her, he shrugged. But the car stayed in the driveway, and the keys stayed on the hall table.

When he opened a bank account for her, she argued vociferously.

"I don't need your money, Michael. I still have some left of what my parents gave me."

Michael glanced up from the stack of papers he'd been making notations on. "It can't be all that much. You'll need more."

"You've given me so much already," she protested. "I don't need the money."

"Use it to buy things for the baby, then. Aren't babies supposed to need all kinds of terribly expensive things?" he suggested vaguely, his attention drifting back to the paperwork at his elbow.

Brittany opened her mouth to continue the argument and then shut it again, fuming silently. In the month since their marriage, she'd learned that arguing with Michael was one of life's more frustrating exercises. He never got angry. He simply stated his viewpoint and then dropped the subject, as if leaving the decision up to her. There was no pressure, no demands. So why did she have the feeling that she was going to end up doing exactly what he thought she should do?

He shut the folder he'd been studying, then he pushed his chair back from the table, reaching for his plate.

"I'll get that," Brittany said.

"It's no bother," he said, intercepting her. "I've got to go check a couple of sites, and I've got some paperwork that will probably keep me in the office most of the afternoon. Is there anything I can get you while I'm in town?"

"No, thank you. I have everything I need." Brittany trailed after him into the kitchen, vowing to break every plate in the house if he tried to wash the dishes before he left. To avoid the necessity for violence, she all but snatched the plate from his hand, standing in front of the sink like a soldier guarding a nuclear power plant.

"I'll take care of the dishes," she said firmly.

Michael's brows rose as if he thought her attitude a little odd. "Okay. I guess I'll get started, then. If there's anything you need—"

"I know. I can call the office and they'll get hold of you. I'm pregnant, Michael, not dying."

"Sorry. I didn't mean to sound like I thought you couldn't take care of yourself." He hesitated a moment and then gave her a half smile. "I'll see you later. Take it easy."

Brittany still hadn't moved when she heard the door shut behind him. Her shoulders slumped as she wandered back into the dining room. The checkbook still lay in the middle of the table.

Why did she argue with him? It was true that the baby was going to need a lot of things. She was going to have to buy some clothes for herself. She was down to one pair of pants she could get into, and those wouldn't even zip all the way up. The few hundred dollars she had left in her own account wasn't going to go very far.

It was just that when she'd married him, she hadn't expected to become an instant parasite, which was what she felt like. The problem with Michael Sinclair was that he was so damned self-sufficient. He didn't *need* anyone or anything.

He didn't need her to cook or to take care of the house. He was capable of doing those things himself. He didn't seem to expect anything of her. He treated her like a cross between a porcelain doll and an old school chum. Friendly, casual and very careful.

In a fit of annoyance, Brittany picked up the checkbook, then threw it against the wall, feeling a twinge of satisfaction when it bounced onto the floor near her feet. If she'd thought about it at all, she would have assumed that there'd be something she could do so that she felt like more of a partner in this arrangement.

Only Michael didn't need her to do anything. She sighed, her anger replaced with a vague depression. Touching the slight rounding of her belly, she bent down and picked up the checkbook. Rather than spend another day staring at the television, she might as well go and get some clothes that fit.

She was really an ungrateful wretch, she thought remorsefully. He had put his entire life on hold for her, and she resented the fact that he didn't seem to need her help. He provided her with a nice home, a car, money. He was polite and never acted as if he expected gratitude from her, and she snapped and snarled at him.

"It's just that he's *so* polite," she mumbled, picking up the rest of the dishes and carrying them into the kitchen. "Doesn't he ever get angry?"

His calm control was so different from Dan's volatility that it was hard to remember that the two of them had been friends. Didn't he sometimes resent her presence? Didn't he sometimes regret what he'd done?

She rinsed the dishes and set them in the dishwasher, her expression thoughtful. Maybe he was trying to avoid making her feel as if she owed him something. Maybe he was trying to make it clear to her that his help came without strings. And here she was bitching and moaning as if he were making her life a misery.

Guilt clutched at her. She'd have to make it up to him. Tonight, she'd cook him a special dinner.

Michael rolled his head against the ache that had settled in the back of his neck. Too many hours spent over a drafting board, too many arguments with contractors who thought they understood the design better than the architect, and too many nights spent lying awake, thinking about Brittany sleeping just down the hall.

He shut the door of the Mustang behind him with a little more force than necessary. It was dark already, and the evening air was chill with a promise of winter to come. The holiday season was just around the corner, and he couldn't remember a year when he'd felt less like celebrating.

He hunched his shoulders inside the sheepskin-lined denim jacket, staring at the lights that spilled from the windows of the house. His house. His home. His wife. Only he couldn't really think of her that way. She was only sort of his wife.

So why was it that he was beginning to feel a definite possessiveness about her? Why was it so hard to remember that she'd only married him because she was carrying his best friend's child?

Mumbling irritably under his breath, he stalked across the lawn to the door. His key was only halfway to the lock when the door was opened from inside. Light and warmth poured out in a welcoming flood. Brittany stood just inside the door, wearing a loose dress in a color he couldn't quite describe, something between gold and green with overtones of both.

"Hi," she said. He blinked in the brilliance of her smile.

"Hi." Still he hesitated on the doorstep, feeling oddly wary.

"Are you going to come in, or are you going to eat your dinner on the porch?" Her question was light and teasing.

"Sorry." He stepped into the hallway, shrugging out

of his jacket. Brittany took it from him before he had a chance to turn toward the coat closet. "Dinner?"

"Don't tell me you're not hungry," she said brightly, shutting the closet door before turning to look at him. "I spent the past two hours in the kitchen."

"I told you I didn't want—"

"I know, I know. You didn't want me to feel like I had to cook for you. But I wanted to do this. I thought we could celebrate tonight."

"'Celebrate'? Celebrate what?" He followed her into the dining room, feeling his wariness grow. They'd achieved a sort of balance the past few weeks. They didn't get too close, didn't rock the boat. He had a feeling that whatever Brittany had planned was going to rock the boat with a vengeance, and he wasn't sure he liked the idea.

"Oh, I don't know. We can celebrate my new wardrobe." She turned from the table, holding out a glass of wine, sweeping her other hand over her dress at the same time. "I have now officially joined the ranks of pregnant people. I bought maternity clothes today."

"You look very nice," he said slowly. She looked more than nice. She looked beautiful. He took a sip of wine, wishing he didn't have to notice just how beautiful she was.

"Or we could celebrate the fact that fall is almost over," she offered, reaching for her own wineglass.

"I didn't think the end of fall was something that people celebrated. Are you supposed to be drinking?"

A flash of irritation showed through the determined good cheer. "Apple juice." She held the glass up to the light so that the golden color was obvious. "I'm taking good care of myself," she said brightly.

"Good." Michael sipped the wine without tasting it.

There was something in her mood that made him uneasy. It was as if she were trying too hard to be bright and cheerful.

"How was your day?"

"It was fine." The look she flashed him told him he was hardly carrying his end of the conversation, and he forced a smile, trying to relax. "How was your day?"

"It was great." If she'd smiled any wider, her cheeks would surely have split. "Not only did I buy some clothes better suited to my girth, I also went to the supermarket and got some groceries."

"You didn't have to do that. I told you I could handle the shopping. I don't want you carrying a lot of heavy bags."

Her smile seemed a little rigid, but it stayed in place. "I made sure none of them were too heavy."

"Good." He stared at his glass. He seemed to be saying "good" an awful lot tonight. It was obvious Brittany was trying to accomplish something with all this good cheer, but he wasn't quite sure what it was, and any disturbance in the status quo made him uneasy.

"I hope you like beef Wellington. I've always wanted to try making it. I thought if we were going to celebrate tonight, we ought to have something special. It should be done in a little while. Why don't we go into the living room until then?"

"Sure." He had the feeling he was failing some sort of test. If he had some idea what it was Brittany wanted, he might have been able to figure out his role. But the least he could do was try to drum up a little enthusiasm.

"Beef Wellington sounds terrific," he said too heartily.

He sat on the sofa while Brittany sat in the chair across from him. he looked at her and she looked at him. It occurred to him that someone should say something, preferably her. But she seemed to have run out of cheerful remarks, and he couldn't seem to think of anything intelligent to offer. The silence stretched. Seeking inspiration, his gaze fell on the fireplace.

"Why don't I light a fire?" He didn't wait for a response. At this point, any action he took had to be better than sitting there like a wax dummy.

Unfortunately, lighting a fire only took a few moments. Once the flames started licking at the kindling, there was really no excuse to continue kneeling on the hearth, unless he wanted to take up fire worship.

Returning to the sofa, he reached for his wineglass and took a healthy swallow before looking at Brittany again. As she stared at the tiny flames, he had the awful impression that she was fighting the urge to cry.

"The weather sure is cooling off," he said loudly. "I guess winter will be here before too long."

*Great. You sound like the weatherman. Couldn't you think of something intelligent to say? Like the fact that she's never looked more beautiful? Or is her hair as soft as it looks?*

"It is getting cold, isn't it?" She didn't take her eyes off the fire. "It's hard to believe how quickly time passes."

Michael swirled the wine in his glass, watching the lights in the cabernet. She was thinking about Dan. The name hovered unspoken between them. Did she think about him often, wonder how her life might have been if he hadn't died?

*Of course she thinks about him, you idiot. She was in love with him—she's carrying his child.*

The thought was unpalatable, and he tossed down most of the wine without tasting it.

"Dinner smells terrific." His tone was too forceful, almost challenging her to disagree, but it snapped her out of the melancholy he sensed creeping over her.

"I'd better go check it," she said.

He followed her into the kitchen a couple of minutes later, for the first time really noticing the beautifully set table in the dining room. She really had gone to a lot of trouble in an attempt to make this a special evening. He'd started off on the wrong foot, but he would do the best he could to try to recapture the mood she'd been trying to set.

That didn't seem likely, however, considering what awaited him in the kitchen. When he walked in, Brittany was staring at the stove, her shoulders slumped, her whole posture indicative of defeat. Sitting in a roasting pan on top of the stove was dinner.

Michael had eaten beef Wellington once or twice, and he was sure it wasn't supposed to look quite the way this one looked. The crust was not the golden brown he recalled. Rather, it was quite dark. Some people might have called it burned, but he wasn't quite so tactless.

"It looks...done."

"It's burned.

"Not really. It's just a little...darker than usual. It looks great."

"Do you really think so?" Once she brightened a little, Michael was determined to eat every centimeter of blackened crust.

"I think it looks wonderful. Why don't I carve it while you serve whatever else it is you've made."

He lifted the roast onto a cutting board and got out

the butcher knife, feeling his spirits lift. There was something very domestic about the scene. Here he was about to carve the roast, and Brittany was putting broccoli into a bowl. It was right out of a Norman Rockwell.

He sliced the end off the roast and the good cheer faded. The meat inside the blackened wrapper was raw. Not rare but raw.

"How does it look?"

He quickly scooped the end slice back into place, holding it there with the knife as Brittany came over to inspect it.

"It's...well..." He groped for something to say. This dinner seemed very important to her. He didn't want to be the one to tell her that it looked as if it needed another hour or so in the oven. "Actually, it may need just a minute or two more in the oven," he said carefully.

"It's not done? Let me see."

Reluctantly, Michael lowered the knife, letting the end slice fall to the cutting board. Brittany stared at the meat in dead silence.

"It's raw."

"Well, not raw, exactly. Just a little too rare."

"It's raw. The crust is burned and the meat is raw." She set the bowl of broccoli on the counter with a crack. "All I wanted to do was cook a decent meal."

"It would only take a little more time in the oven, and I'm sure it would be fine."

"Don't patronize me, Michael."

"I'm not patronizing you. If we just put the roast back in the oven and cook it awhile longer, it will be fine."

"Right. We cook it until the crust actually turns to charcoal instead of just coming close."

"So, we peel the crust off."

"I don't want to peel the damned crust off," she snapped furiously. "All I wanted was to cook a simple meal, sit down and enjoy it."

"Beef Wellington is hardly a simple meal." He'd intended to offer consolation, but it wasn't taken that way.

"Right! I should have tackled a nice simple frozen lasagna. Is that what you're trying to say?"

"No. I just meant—"

"I don't care what you meant. I know you think I'm a helpless idiot." She shoved past him, snatching up the roast and throwing it into the sink, jabbing it with a fork in a vain attempt to make the entire piece of meat disappear down the garbage disposal.

Michael looked on in confusion. He'd obviously done something to upset her but, for the life of him, he couldn't figure out what. Maybe this was one of those mood swings pregnant women were supposed to experience. He watched her furious attack on the roast for a moment before venturing a comment.

"I don't think that will go down the disposal that way."

Brittany spun away from the sink, the fork held like a weapon in her hand. "I'm perfectly capable of running a garbage disposal."

"Okay. Sorry." He lifted his hands, palm out. His acquiescence only seemed to make her madder.

"Don't you ever get mad?" She didn't give him a chance to answer, turning back to continue her attack on the roast. "Why should you bother to get mad at me? You probably don't think I'm worth it."

"You're not making any sense, Brittany."

"Of course I'm not. Poor, stupid Brittany. She can't manage anything on her own."

"Would you stop this?"

If she hadn't been so engrossed in her own emotional turmoil, she might have heard the edge in Michael's voice. But all the frustration and helplessness of the past few months had finally come to a boil. There was no stopping the torrent now that she'd started.

"You think I can't manage anything. After all, I was stupid enough to get pregnant. You can hardly blame me for Dan's death, but I undoubtedly didn't manage things too well after that, did I? I bet you pat yourself on the back every night for coming to my rescue. You're so damned noble. So bloody self-sufficient." She jabbed furiously at the uncooperative roast, oblivious to the taut silence behind her.

"Well, maybe I'm not as good at taking care of myself as you are. But I'm damned if I'll stay here, damned if I'll let you make me feel like a helpless child. You can take your charity and stuff it—Oh!"

She broke off on a gasp as Michael's hand closed over her upper arm, spinning her away from the sink. At first glance he looked no different than he usually did...until she saw his eyes. Anger darkened them to almost black, and the hand that held her arm was not hurtful, but it was far from gentle.

"I think you've said just about enough," he suggested. The quiet tone restored the voice that surprise had stolen from her.

"Let go of me."

"Shut up." He used his grip on her arm to pull her closer. "You've been babbling on for the past five minutes, making very little sense."

"It all makes perfect sense," she muttered mutinously.

"Do you really think that I pat myself on the back for helping you? That I think you're helpless?"

"Well, you act that way."

"How do I act that way? Explain to me what I'm doing to give you the notion that I think so little of you."

"You treat me like I can't reason for myself. You're always telling me to take care of myself, questioning whether or not I should be drinking wine or vacuuming the floor or dressing myself."

"Did it occur to you that I might be concerned?"

"Of course you're concerned. After you've made all these noble sacrifices for me, I'm sure you're concerned."

He drew her even closer, leaning down until only inches separated their faces, his eyes blazing directly into hers. "If you say one more word about my 'noble sacrifice,' I swear I'm not going to be responsible for my actions."

He paused but Brittany had run out of words. She'd wondered if he had a temper, although now that she was seeing it up close, she decided that she'd rather not push him any further. Not that she thought he'd do her any physical injury. Still, he looked more than a little intimidating.

"I didn't make any noble sacrifices when I married you. I married you because I wanted to. I wanted to help you, and I felt like I owed it to Dan."

"You thought I was a helpless nitwit," she muttered to his shirtfront.

"No, I didn't. Even though you'd gone through some rough times, I thought you'd come out pretty damned good. Just because you need a little help doesn't mean you're a nitwit.''

"Then why do you act like you think I'm helpless?" She lifted her eyes to his, her anger gone but not the hurt she felt. "You're all the time telling me not to lift things or move anything. I feel like I can hardly breathe.''

"I just don't want you to hurt yourself." His fingers dropped from her arm.

"You make me feel like I'm too stupid to take care of myself, like if you're not there to watch over me every minute, I'm going to do something dumb.''

"I don't mean to do that." Michael looked away, thrusting his fingers through his hair.

"Then why do you? Do you think I'm helpless?"

"No, of course not," he said impatiently.

"Then why?"

The silence stretched out until Brittany wondered if he was going to answer. When he spoke at last, his voice was husky. "About a month before Dan...before Dan was killed, my mother had a miscarriage.''

"Oh, Michael, I didn't know.''

"They really wanted that baby. It hurt her terribly. Dad finally took her on a cruise to try and get her mind off it. She took good care of herself, but she lost the baby anyway." He shrugged. "I guess if I'm a little overprotective of you, maybe that's why.''

"Oh, Michael." Brittany wondered if it were possible to simply slither into a corner somewhere and melt away. She'd been so sure that his attitude toward her had nothing to do with anyone but her. It hadn't even occurred to her that it might have a basis in something totally unrelated. All these weeks she'd been so angry and frustrated.

"It must have been very difficult for your mother."

"It was rough." The simple statement told her as much as any lengthy explanation of what Beth had suffered.

"I'm sorry I acted like a shrew."

"I'm sorry if I was smothering you."

Silence settled awkwardly between them. The kitchen seemed suddenly much too quiet. Brittany laughed uneasily. "I guess we just had our first fight."

"I guess we did."

"I guess maybe we're really married now."

Michael half smiled, his eyes shadowed. "More or less. Do I really make you feel stupid?"

Brittany shrugged. "Not really. You just seem so self-sufficient. I guess I feel a little useless around here."

"I didn't marry you so you could be useful."

"I know, but I'd feel better if there was something I could do."

"Like what?"

"I don't know," she admitted. "But something. I can't just sit around for the next five months twiddling my thumbs."

"Aren't there things you need to do to prepare for the baby?" he questioned with some vague image of her knitting booties.

"Nothing that's going to take up all my time."

"Well, there must be things around here. What about cooking?" His eyes fell on the mangled roast that lay pathetically in the sink. "Maybe not."

Brittany laughed, feeling as if a weight had lifted. They were talking. Really talking. The quarrel seemed to have used up the tension that had been building between them.

"Don't you trust my culinary expertise?"

"Well, I wouldn't put it that way, exactly. Let's just say that I wouldn't want to depend on you to keep us from starving to death."

"Coward."

"You didn't see how dangerous you looked with that fork in your hand," he teased.

"Speaking of food…" She looked at the roast, suddenly aware that she was hungry.

"I'm starving. A friend of my parents' has opened a new Mexican restaurant."

"I love Mexican food."

That evening marked a turning point in their marriage. It was as if, by surviving their first quarrel, they'd established a relationship separate from the events that had brought them together. Brittany and Michael had formed a rapport that was not dependent on the relationships they'd had with Dan.

It was, as Beth had told her, impossible to live with someone and not become involved with them. A marriage license tied them together, but it was more than that. There was a bond there, and with each day that passed, it grew stronger.

"Brittany, I'm so glad you could join me for lunch." Beth's smile was welcoming as Brittany settled into the chair across from her and took a menu from the waiter.

"It isn't like my schedule is heavily booked these days. Most of my friends are in school."

"It gets lonely, doesn't it? I felt as if I'd fallen into some kind of black hole where no one knew I existed anymore."

There was such feeling in the words that Brittany looked over the top of her menu, her eyes curious.

"You sound like you know what it's like."

"I do. I was younger than you are, only sixteen, when I quit school."

"You quit because you were pregnant?" The menu was forgotten.

"I was pregnant with Michael. In those days, there was no question of my staying in high school. Heaven knows, I might have contaminated the other girls." She laughed, her eyes sparkling with amusement, but it didn't take psychic ability to know that it must have been painful at the time.

Brittany hesitated, her eyes dropping to the table. In the two months since she and Michael had been married, Beth and Donovan had never by word or look made her feel less than a member of the family. At Thanksgiving, she'd been welcomed as if she and Michael had a real marriage, as if the child she carried were his.

Still, she sensed a slight barrier between her and her in-laws. She knew Beth feared that Michael was going to end up hurt. Perhaps they also feared growing too close to her or to the child she carried. After all, she wasn't going to be part of their lives forever, as they might expect a real daughter-in-law to be.

She stirred in her seat, uncomfortable with the thought of a *real* daughter-in-law, a real wife for Michael. She'd grown accustomed to thinking that he belonged to her, even if it was only for a few months.

"Brittany?" Beth's voice snapped her out of her thoughts, and she looked up to see the waiter standing next to the table. Flustered, she asked for a chef's salad, hoping there was such a thing on the menu. Since he didn't question the order, she assumed she hadn't revealed her total unfamiliarity with the menu.

"You looked like you were miles away," Beth commented when the waiter was gone.

"Not really. I was thinking that it must have been very hard for you, being so young and all."

"It wasn't easy but I had Donovan." The way she said it made it impossible to doubt that that had been enough. "And you have Michael."

"I don't know where I'd have been without him," Brittany admitted.

"The two of you seem to be settling in quite well." If there was a touch of maternal anxiety in the words, Brittany could hardly blame her.

"It took a little bit of adjusting, but we're doing all right. You know, I've thought a lot about what you said—about the fact that a marriage has a certain life of its own."

"Goodness, did I say that? How pompous of me." Beth leaned back as the waiter brought their salads.

Brittany waited until he was gone again before continuing. "It wasn't pompous. It was very true. I mean, even though Michael and I don't have a real marriage, there's a definite bond between us. Maybe it's because we were sort of friends before this, but we've made some adjustments and learned to talk to each other more openly. We've even had a quarrel or two. We've learned to compromise."

"What do you think a real marriage is, Brittany?" Beth asked gently. "A real marriage is all about compromise, about each of you giving a little and taking a little. There are so many ties that come with living together day to day. Don't make the mistake of thinking that either of you is going to be able to walk away from this without hurt."

Beth's words lingered in Brittany's mind long after

the lunch was over. Walking along the street, past shop windows full of Christmas displays, she thought about it. Ties. She hadn't expected to feel tied to Michael. Gratitude, affection maybe, but not this feeling that their lives were bound together.

She stopped in front of a toy store window, looking in at the displays. Next year at this time, she'd be shopping for her son or daughter. And she'd be shopping alone. The thought slipped in unbidden, causing a surprising ache in her chest.

It was getting harder and harder to think of the time when Michael would no longer be a daily part of her life. But that had been the plan from the start. He'd only married her because she was carrying Dan's child. Once that child was born and she'd had a chance to get on her feet again, the time would come to break those ties.

Dan. She closed her eyes, trying to picture his face, but the image was fuzzy around the edges. The eyes showed a tendency to darken from Dan's icy blue to Michael's sky blue. She couldn't make the hair stay sun-streaked brown. It was darker, richer. And the face... Why couldn't she call the face more sharply to mind?

Hands shaking, she dug in her purse for her wallet, snapping it open to the picture of Dan. Yes. That was it. He was laughing into the camera. How could she have forgotten the way his eyes laughed? She stroked her thumb over the photograph, feeling tears fill her eyes.

Things would have been so different if he'd lived. *But would they have been better?*

She hushed the tiny voice, closing the wallet and tucking it back into her purse. She'd loved Dan. Nothing was going to change that. Nothing. And no one.

# Chapter Seven

Christmas arrived with a snowfall worthy of a post-card. Remembrance became an enchanted town, full of beautiful drifts of white.

Michael drove the Mustang slowly along the icy streets. Brittany watched the houses along the way, unaware of the quick look he shot her from time to time.

"Something wrong?" he finally asked.

"No." She turned her head, conjuring up a smile. "Should there be?"

"You look…sad." He braked carefully at a stop sign before turning to look at her, his eyes searching. "You don't like Christmas?"

"I love Christmas." She smoothed her hand over the soft wool of her coat. "I was just thinking about my parents. Wondering if they think about me."

Michael felt a familiar surge of anger at the thought of her parents. Brittany rarely mentioned them, but he knew their absence in her life was a source of hurt. Personally, he thought they were no loss. Remembering the woman who'd so coolly told him that she had no idea where her daughter was, all he felt was a strong desire to go back and give her a piece of his mind. But he supposed Brittany might feel differently.

"You could call them," he suggested evenly, keeping his own feelings out of his voice. "Tell them you're married."

"No." She shook her head. "I miss them but if they can't put me ahead of the opinions of other people, then I won't go crawling to them."

"You wouldn't have to crawl. A phone call would probably do." He thought she was well rid of them. Why was he arguing in their favor? Because he hated seeing the sadness in her eyes.

"No. They made their choice. Besides, I don't think they're the kind of people I want influencing my child. I don't want my son or daughter growing up thinking that other people's opinions are more important than love and loyalty."

Since he wholeheartedly agreed with her, there was really nothing Michael could say in argument. They finished the rest of the drive in silence.

The gathering at Beth and Donovan's was small. Just the family and Carol Montgomery, who Brittany had learned was as close to family as it was possible to get. She and Beth had been friends since childhood. Brittany liked Carol, with her slightly acerbic wit and dry practicality. She didn't know if Carol knew the truth about her marriage. If she did, she'd never shown it.

Presents were unwrapped before the late afternoon meal. Brittany had spent a considerable amount of time trying to decide what to get her in-laws. It had to be something personal but not too personal, hovering somewhere between a gift a real daughter-in-law might give and a gift a near stranger might give. In the end she'd settled on a delicate silk scarf for Beth, the floral print swirling across a peacock-blue background.

Donovan had been much more difficult. He was more reserved, harder to know. At first she'd thought it was only with her that he showed that unapproachable air, but she'd realized that it was a natural part of his makeup. Desperation had finally driven her to pick up her knitting needles three weeks before Christmas. The sweater was a simple pullover, but she'd chosen the yarn with great care, trying to find something that matched his green-gold eyes.

She'd been pleased with the results until she saw him opening the box. Now that the moment was at hand, she was sure that the gift had been much too personal. Besides, he probably hated sweaters. Donovan reached into the box, drawing the sweater out, studying it silently while Brittany held her breath.

"She made it," Michael told him, ignoring Brittany's squeak of protest.

Donovan's eyes left the sweater to settle on her. "You made this yourself?"

She nodded, sure that he was going to hate it even more than he already did now that he knew she'd made it.

"If you don't like it..." she began weakly.

"It's beautiful, Brittany." The quiet words seemed utterly sincere. He stripped off the sweater he'd been wearing and pulled the one she'd made him on over his shirt. The fit was perfect and Brittany felt a small glow of pride. She'd judged his size by Michael's. Donovan tugged the sweater into place and then looked at her again.

"Thank you." He smiled at her, the first time he'd really smiled at her, and Brittany felt her heart bump.

It wasn't hard to see why Beth looked at him as if the sun rose and set on him. When he smiled like that, it was hard to imagine *not* falling in love with him.

"You're welcome," she murmured, her eyes dropping to the package she held.

"Well, it's a sure bet this is the first handmade sweater you've ever gotten, Donovan." That was Carol, her tone lightly acerbic. "The last time Beth picked up a pair of knitting needles, it looked like she was knitting a hat for Godzilla." She paused, her expression considering. "Come to think of it, Godzilla is a better dresser than that."

Beth threw a wad of wrapping paper at her friend, and everyone laughed, the small moment of tension forgotten. But Donovan left the sweater on, and every time she saw it, Brittany felt as if she were truly a part of the family.

While Beth and Carol squabbled over Beth's skills of the needle or lack thereof, Michael unearthed a small box from under a mound of wrapping paper.

Brittany's eyes met his, as he handed it to her and she wondered if it was her imagination that read uncertainty in his gaze. Was it possible that he was as nervous as she?

"I wasn't sure what to get you, but when I saw this, I thought of you."

She took the package from him, aware of the subtle tingle when her fingers touched his. Slipping the bright red wrapping paper from the box, she held a plain blue jeweler's case, the firm's name discreetly embossed on the lid in gold.

She glanced up at Michael but could read little from his expression. Taking a deep breath, she snapped open the case and felt the air leave her when she saw the delicate band of sparkling jewels lying on the dark velvet background.

"Oh!" The only word she could get out.

"If you don't like it, we can exchange it," Michael offered when the silence stretched.

"Not like it!" Brittany's fingers tightened over the case. "I'd have to be crazy not to like it. It's absolutely gorgeous. But it's too much."

"You can't have it both ways. Either it's gorgeous or it's too much."

Glancing up, she caught the teasing light in his eyes, and she smiled reluctantly.

"It's perfect but it's much too expensive. You shouldn't have spent so much money."

"Did I ever tell you that I hate people telling me what I should or shouldn't do?" he asked conversationally. He reached out to take the box from her hand, lifting the bracelet from its bed of velvet. "Hold out your hand."

Staring at the bracelet, Brittany reminded herself of all the reasons she couldn't possibly accept a gift like this from Michael. It wouldn't be right. She'd insist that he return it.

Her hand lifted and she watched as Michael clasped the bracelet around her wrist. It felt cool against her skin, yet it seemed afire with light. The contrast was oddly seductive. Michael held her hand as he studied the sparkling diamonds.

"It suits you. I knew it would when I saw it."

That was all he said, but there was something in the tone of his voice that brought a flush to Brittany's cheeks.

Twisting the bracelet around and around on her wrist, she watched, as Donovan lifted an enormous box

from under the tree, then set it in front of Michael. It
had seemed like such a good idea when she saw the
ad. Now, she wasn't so sure. Just because he'd admired
an antique train set in a store didn't mean he actually
wanted one. It had cost her virtually every cent she had
left of her own money.

The man she'd bought the set from had inherited it
from his uncle who'd once worked on the railroads.
Every car was in the box it had come in.

Michael didn't say a word when he saw what the
box held. Brittany was acutely aware that everyone was
watching. They probably couldn't believe she'd actually done something so stupid. Who bought train sets
for a grown man? She finally couldn't stand the silence
another moment.

"There's more track. I couldn't get it all in the box.
As it was, your father had to carry it in for me." She
watched nervously as he lifted one of the cars out, sliding it from its box and studying the construction. "I
wasn't sure… You liked one you saw in a toy store. I
thought you might like one of your own…" She trailed
off, feeling like a total idiot. How could she have been
so dumb?

Michael slipped the car carefully back into its box
before looking at her. It wasn't annoyance or disap-
pointment she saw in his eyes.

"It's wonderful, Brittany." The quiet sincerity in his
words brought a foolish flood of tears to her eyes, and
she looked down to conceal them. "I don't think I've
ever gotten a gift I liked more. Thank you."

"You're welcome." She couldn't think of anything
more to say, though it seemed as though there should
be something.

The silence might have grown awkward, but Beth

broke it by standing up. "I don't know about anybody else, but all this greed has made me hungry."

Dinner was a Christmas celebration like Brittany had always thought they should be. Her own parents had tended toward a formal meal with a few close friends from their church. The main focus had always been the importance of being grateful for the good things that had happened in the past year.

At the Sinclair home, the main requirement seemed to be that there was plenty of laughter and plenty of food. They gave thanks by showing their joy in their lives and each other. It seemed a more fitting celebration.

Brittany couldn't put her finger on quite what it was, but there seemed to have been some subtle shift in her relationship with Beth and Donovan. Maybe it was the holiday spirit. Maybe it was the fact that her gift to Michael had clearly meant a great deal to him. Whatever it was, that subtle barrier seemed to have come down. She no longer felt like a visitor in their lives; she felt a part of the family.

If she'd had any lingering doubts about Michael's pleasure in her gift, they were dissolved when he and Donovan began setting up the track immediately after supper. They squabbled good-naturedly over how it should be done, ignoring Beth's mild protest when they decided that the only suitable place was the middle of the living room floor. Donovan gave his wife an absent kiss, telling her that they'd be careful not to make a mess. Brittany couldn't help but giggle at the way Beth rolled her eyes.

The two men crawled around on the floor, hooking track together, mumbling about transformers and currents. The women sat near the fire, talking in a desultory fashion, watching the antics of the supposed adults on the floor.

When the track was at last pronounced ready, everything else came to a halt while the switch was thrown, promptly plunging the room into darkness. There was a moment of stunned silence, and then Beth giggled. Even in the firelight it was possible to see the disgruntled look Donovan threw her, and Brittany bit her cheek, trying not to laugh out loud.

"Good thing you guys aren't running a major railroad," Carol said.

Muttering about transformers and fuses and overloaded circuits, Michael and Donovan trooped down to the basement. Light was restored a few minutes later, and a short time after that, the train was ready for another test run.

"Shall I get some candles?" Beth asked politely when informed that it was time to throw the switch. The look Donovan shot her promised retribution, but she didn't look worried. Everyone held their breath while the switch was thrown, but the lights remained on and the train began to move.

From the look on Michael's face, it could have been the first transcontinental train. He glanced up at Brittany with a bright boyish grin, sharing the moment with her. She smiled at him, unaware of the fact that Beth was watching the two of them, a faint frown in the back of her eyes.

Carol left not long after the triumph with the train. More snow was predicted, and she wanted to get home before the storm. After she was gone, Beth announced that Donovan could help her with the dishes. Brittany offered to help, but Beth waved her back into her seat.

"You stay there. Let the mighty engineer do something useful, for a change."

"That's right, make fun of me. My ego can take it." Donovan's long-suffering tone didn't match the laughter in his eyes. He slid his arm around Beth's waist, leaning down to murmur something in her ear. Whatever it was, she blushed and laughed as he led her from the room.

Brittany leaned her head against the back of the sofa, watching as Michael sent the train circling around and around the track. The motion was hypnotic, and she closed her eyes, letting herself drift contentedly in a state somewhere between waking and sleeping.

She opened her eyes slowly when she felt the cushion next to her dip. The train still circled lazily around the track, but Michael was sitting beside her, his eyes on the slow movement.

"Are you tired?" he asked.

"A little. It was a nice day. Probably the nicest Christmas I've ever had."

"I'm glad." He looked at her, wondering if she had any idea of how utterly beautiful she was. She'd left her hair down, clipping it back from her face with a pair of bright red combs that matched the softer wool of her dress. Her eyes were soft in the firelight. She looked drowsy and contented. And so desirable.

He wanted to take her in his arms and kiss her, feel her mouth soften under his, her arms steal around his neck. He looked away, surprised by the intensity of the urge.

A startled gasp brought his gaze back to her. She was looking at him, her eyes wide, one hand pressed to the mound of her stomach. His heart bumped with panic.

"What is it? What's wrong?"

"Nothing." She laughed unsteadily. "Nothing's wrong. The baby just moved."

"Moved?" His eyes dropped to her stomach.

"Here. Feel it." She reached for his hand, pressing it against her rounded tummy. Michael started to draw back, uneasy. He froze when he felt a sudden quick pressure against his hand. His eyes lifted to Brittany's, sharing the wonder.

"He's kicking," she said quietly.

"It could be a girl," he reminded her, a slow smile breaking when he felt the movement again. "Does it hurt?"

"No, it feels...funny. It makes it real, somehow. There's a person in there, someone totally new."

Michael's eyes dropped to where his hand rested against her belly. Until now, he'd rarely thought of the child she carried, and when he did, it hadn't been as a real, living being. Her pregnancy had been the catalyst for their marriage, the reason for all the upheaval in both their lives. Beyond that, he'd given it little thought.

Suddenly, the child she carried was real. It was something more than merely the instrument that had brought them together. It was a person, a human being in its own right.

When the child kicked again, he looked up at Brittany, grinning. "Feels like he's going to be a football player."

"Or she." Her smile matched his.

Without realizing, in that moment, Michael became as much a father to the child Brittany carried as Dan could have been. The conception hadn't been his, but the child suddenly was.

So absorbed were they in the miracle of the moment that neither of them noticed that Beth and Donovan had come into the room. When Beth turned away, Donovan followed her, catching up with her in the dining room.

She was standing at the window, staring out at the snow that was just starting to drift down, her hands clasping her elbows. When he stopped behind her, she leaned back, her head resting on his shoulder. In the light reflected off the snow, he could see the gleam of a solitary tear on her cheek.

"Does it still hurt so much?" he asked, wrapping his arms around her, wishing he could take away her pain.

"Not always. Most of the time I don't think about it. It's just that it's Christmas. Our baby was due about now. This might have been her first Christmas." Her voice broke on the words, and she turned, burying her face against his shoulder.

"Don't cry, sweetheart. You know the doctor said we could try again." He stroked his hand over her hair.

"I'm too old."

"No, you're not. Lots of women older than you are have babies."

"But what if I can't?" She lifted her face from his shoulder, looking up at him searchingly.

"Beth, having another child with you would be wonderful, but I don't need that to make me happy." A touch of anger flared in the back of his eyes. "You shouldn't have to ask that."

"I know. But sometimes I wonder."

They were quiet for a few moments, Beth held safe in Donovan's arms, his gaze on the snowy world outside.

"Does it bother you, watching Brittany?" he asked at last.

"Once in a while." She stirred, turning in his arms so that his hands were linked in front of her and she could look out the window. "They remind me so much of us when we first got married. They're so young and so sure that they can make life do what they want it to. I'm afraid they're going to end up hurt."

"There's not much we can do about it."

"I know but I can't help but worry." She tilted her head back until their eyes met. "I love you, Donovan. I love you so much."

He looked down at her with so much love in his eyes she didn't need the words he gave her.

"I love you, Beth. I always will."

Christmas had marked another subtle turning point in Brittany's marriage. She and Michael had drawn closer together. In some way she didn't quite understand, they were becoming a couple, just as Beth had predicted. There was a new ease between them, a casual intimacy that she found unnerving when she thought about it.

It was sometimes hard to remember the reasons behind this marriage, hard to remember that it wasn't a real marriage. Every night, when she climbed into her solitary bed, she was reminded of those reasons. But when she was with Michael, they became distant, foggy things that didn't seem quite real.

It wasn't that she was falling in love with him. Dan was certainly the only man she would ever love—there could be no doubt about that. With Michael, it was more a case of falling in like. How could you not like a man who thought Laurel and Hardy were the funniest comedians of all time, who considered a banana split the height of culinary achievement and who never once made her feel as if marrying her had caused him the slightest moment's doubt?

No, she'd never love again, but with Michael she was discovering that life could be full again, that she could be happy.

"I want some popcorn." Brittany's announcement came just as John Wayne was dismounting, preparatory to stalking through the milling cattle in search of Montgomery Clift.

"You can't leave now," Michael protested. "This is the big finale."

"I've seen *Red River* at least five times. I think I can remember the finale. Besides, we can always run the tape back."

Michael rolled his eyes. "It's not the same. If you want to wait a minute, I'll make the popcorn."

"That's okay. If I don't move soon, I'm going to sink into the sofa permanently."

Michael might have argued further, but John Ireland had just called John Wayne's name. Brittany shook her head as she stood up and went into the kitchen. She smoothed a hand over her belly beneath one of Michael's old shirts. At six and a half months there was no longer any way to conceal her condition.

Reaching for the popcorn, she smiled. In the living room, she could hear the sound of fighting. There'd be no peeling Michael away from the set until the last of the credits had rolled. John Wayne movies were a not-so-secret vice of his.

She poured a thin layer of oil in the bottom of the pan, waiting for it to heat before adding the popcorn.

It was only after she'd added the golden kernels that she realized she didn't have a lid handy. Muttering at her lack of planning, she lowered herself to search through the bottom cabinets.

The lid proved more elusive than she'd hoped. She was halfway into a cabinet when she realized that if she didn't turn the popcorn off, it was going to end up all over the kitchen. She backed awkwardly out of the cabinet, but she lifted her head too soon, banging it solidly against the frame, startling a cry of pain out of her as she collapsed on the floor.

She'd barely had a chance to lift a hand to her throbbing head when Michael showed up, drawn by her cry.

"What happened? Are you all right?" He was on his knees beside her, concern darkening his eyes.

"I hit my head."

"Did you fall? Do you feel dizzy? Sick?"

"No, no and no. I was looking for a lid, and I tried to stand up before I was out of the cabinet. Help me up, please."

"Are you sure you should stand up? Maybe you should just stay where you are for a few minutes."

"Michael, I'm not going to stay sprawled on the kitchen floor like some obese kitchen witch. I just bumped my head." Her tone was mildly exasperated. She'd come to accept that he couldn't control his overprotective streak.

He stood up reluctantly, taking her hands and lifting her to her feet. Brittany was grateful for the help. Standing up these days wasn't as simple as it had been. Michael released her hands but didn't move away, and she knew at the slightest sign of dizziness, he'd have her wrapped safe in his arms. She had to admit that there was a certain comfort in that knowledge.

She reached up to try to judge the extent of the damage to her head, but Michael's hand was there first.

"Let me see." His fingers were gentle at the back of her head, but when he touched the place she'd hit, she sucked in a quick breath.

"Sorry."

"That's okay. It's just a little tender." She lifted her eyes to his face, half smiling. "What do you think, Doc? Will I live?"

"I don't think the skin is broken, but you're going to have a bit of a lump. Are you sure you feel okay?"

"I feel fine. You want to check to see if my pupils are dilated and reactive? That's what they do on all the best hospital shows."

"I'm not sure I'd know what a dilated pupil looked like." He looked at her eyes, his hand lingering in her hair. "You really should be more careful." But he wasn't thinking about the bump on her head. He was wondering how it was possible that she could be so beautiful.

Maybe it was true that pregnant women took on a special glow. Brittany seemed lighted from within. He lifted a hand to her cheek, stroking the impossibly soft skin. Her eyes widened in surprise.

For months he'd forced himself to pretend that he felt nothing but friendship for her, that the fact that she was his wife meant nothing. Now, with his hand tangled in her hair, that suddenly seemed such a foolish waste.

His head lowered, his mouth catching Brittany's surprised little gasp. It was the first time he'd kissed her since that stilted little moment at the wedding. Her mouth was softer than he remembered, opening beneath his like a flower drinking in the sun.

There was none of the hesitation that went with a first kiss. They were married; they'd lived together for months. There were bonds of intimacy between them that flared to life the moment he kissed her.

Brittany's hands came to rest on his chest, hesitating there a moment before sliding up to his shoulders. Desire flared in the pit of his stomach, and his arm dropped to her back, drawing her closer.

He felt as if he could absorb her into his skin, make her a part of himself. His mouth slanted across hers, and Brittany's arms tightened around his neck. The need he felt was so immediate, so basic that it left no room for thought. He'd wanted this for so long, from the moment he'd first met her.

There was a sudden small pressure where her rounded belly was pressed against his hip. He ignored it, his arms pulling her still closer, his mouth hungry on hers. The pressure came again, tugging at the fog he wanted to draw between them and reality. It felt as if someone was kicking him. He felt the movement again and dragged his mouth from Brittany's, suddenly aware of what he was doing.

The baby. The baby was moving within her, as if in protest of what was happening. His arms dropped away from her, and he took a step back. Brittany swayed as if the abrupt end to the embrace had thrown her off balance. Michael reached out, steadying her with a hand at her elbow, drawing back from even that small contact the moment he was sure she didn't need the support.

"I'm sorry." He couldn't meet her eyes, focusing his gaze on the floor between them, one hand shoved into his pocket, the other clenching and unclenching at his side.

Brittany stared at him, still dazed by the unexpected flare of passion.

"I'm sorry. I didn't mean—I had no right—" He broke off, his jaw tight.

What was he talking about? She lifted a hand to push her hair back, trying to corral her scattered thoughts into order. Why was he apologizing?

"Michael." The husky sound of her voice surprised her, and she cleared her throat before she continued. "Michael, there's nothing to apologize for. You didn't attack me." She waited but he didn't smile, didn't look at her. He just stood there, a muscle ticking in his jaw and that hand clenching and unclenching. She tried again.

"We *are* married." That got a reaction, but not the one she'd expected.

"That's not why I married you," he said fiercely. "This was never supposed to be anything more than a marriage in name only. That's what we agreed to. It was never supposed to be a real marriage."

Brittany drew in a sharp breath, hurt flowering inside her at his sharp words. *Never supposed to be a real marriage.* Funny, she almost never thought of that anymore. Somewhere along the line, it had begun to seem pretty real to her. But apparently she was alone in that feeling.

Michael might want her—she knew that much—but he had no intention of getting any more involved with her. Did he think she might try to hang on to him if they made this a *real* marriage?

Hurt filled her throat, making it impossible to speak. Without a word, she walked by him and out of the room. A moment later, Michael heard the door of her room shut. His shoulders slumped.

How could he have been such a fool? He'd spent months walking a carefully balanced line. They'd established a relationship that was close but not too close, friendly but not too friendly. If he'd occasionally wanted more than that, he'd squashed the thought.

All it had taken was the feel of Brittany's hair against his fingers to show just how fragile that balance was. The feel of her mouth under his, the way she'd responded to him... He groaned and shoved his fingers through his hair, trying to shut the memory away.

She'd responded. But that didn't mean that she'd felt the same things he'd felt. She felt grateful to him. He knew that. How was it possible to separate that gratitude from whatever else she might feel? He didn't want her to come to him because she felt she owed it to him—to repay a debt.

He groaned again, rubbing at the ache that had started to throb in his temples. Why wasn't anything simple anymore?

As if in response to his silent inquiry, loud popping sounds broke the quiet, and fluffy white kernels of popcorn began exploding out of the uncovered pan on the stove.

Cursing, Michael turned the burner off, but the residual heat kept the process going, and in a matter of seconds, puffy spots of white were dotting the counters and floor.

He set the pan in the sink, then he just stared at the mess, wondering if this was a silent commentary on the current state of his life.

# Chapter Eight

Michael came awake suddenly, startled from sleep by some sound he couldn't quite remember. He sat up, swinging his legs out of bed, his first thought—as it so often was—of Brittany. She'd been so uncomfortable this past couple of weeks.

And she'd been particularly uncomfortable tonight. Not that she'd said anything, but he'd seen it in the way she'd shifted restlessly in her seat, trying to find some position that relieved the ache in her back.

The baby was due in two weeks, but he sometimes wondered how she could bear the discomfort for much longer. The bloom that had marked the earlier months of her pregnancy had faded. She looked pale and worn. When he'd pressed, she'd admitted that she wasn't sleeping well, but she'd insisted that this was a normal phase of pregnancy. She just had a hard time getting comfortable.

He was halfway into the hallway when he heard the sound again. This time he knew what it was, and his heart started to beat faster. He covered the distance to

Brittany's door in three quick strides, pushing it open without bothering to knock. She was half in and half out of bed, her head bent forward, her hands pressed to her stomach as she took quick, shallow breaths. Despite her efforts, a tiny whimper of pain escaped—the sound that had awakened him.

The pain eased as he knelt beside her, and she lifted her head to look at him, her eyes wide in her pale face. She'd turned on the lamp next to the bed, making it easy to read the fear in her eyes.

"Michael?" His name was all she could manage.

"I'm here." Was that his voice? He sounded so calm. "How far apart are the pains?"

"I'm not sure." She looked at the clock as if she could read the answer there. "Ten minutes, maybe."

"Why didn't you call me?" He reached around her, plumping up the pillows before taking her hands and easing her back against them.

"I didn't want to bother you."

"Don't be silly. Isn't this what I spent all those weeks in training for?" He didn't wait for an answer, disappearing into the bathroom and coming back out with a damp washcloth. Brittany sighed with pleasure as the cool cloth stroked her forehead.

"That feels nice."

"Of course it does." He pushed her hair back from her face. "This is what I learned in boot camp."

"Boot camp?"

"All those classes we took. Did you think I spent all that time practicing with pillows and breathing like a fish just to be robbed of the chance to use it when the time came? Ms. Olafson would be sorely disappointed in me if I failed after all the hours she spent barking orders at us."

"She didn't bark," Brittany protested drowsily. "She was very nice."

"To those among us with large stomachs, maybe." Michael put down the washcloth and stretched out an arm to grab the hairbrush that lay on the dresser. "You don't know how brutal she was on the husbands."

He began to pull the brush through her hair, easing her forward with a hand behind her back so that he could brush the hair up off the nape of her neck.

"Somehow I doubt that."

"You didn't see the way she looked at me," he insisted. "I was shaking in my boots."

She leaned against him, letting the rhythmic stroking of the brush lull her. The nonsensical conversation helped distract her.

"I don't think you've ever been afraid of anyone in your life."

"Only Ms. Olafson," he assured her. "She was—"

He broke off as Brittany's fingers suddenly clutched at his arm, another contraction rippling through her. Michael dropped the brush, catching her hands in his.

"Look at me and breathe. Remember your breathing. Concentrate."

Her eyes clinging to his, Brittany inhaled and panted, following his instructions. She lay back when the contraction eased, but she didn't release his hands.

"I'm scared, Michael," she admitted shakily. "What if something goes wrong?"

"Nothing is going to go wrong," he promised her. "In a few hours, we're going to have a beautiful son or daughter."

She didn't even notice his automatic use of "we're." Now that the time was here, she was suddenly filled with doubts and fears.

"But—" His finger across her lips stopped her before she could even get the words out.

"No 'buts' about it. Everything is going to be fine, Brittany."

"You won't leave me?" She was beyond caring that her tone was openly pleading. In the past few months, Michael had been the one steady thing in her life.

"I won't leave you. Breathe."

A few minutes later, he slanted a quick look at the clock as another contraction took her. When it had eased, he lifted her gently.

"The contractions are about five minutes apart," he said in answer to her protesting moan. "I think we should get you to the hospital."

"Oh!" The exclamation made him freeze.

"What is it? Another contraction?"

"No. I think my water just broke." She looked up at him, her expression a mixture of fear and embarrassment. "I'm sorry. I've been so much trouble. Since the very beginning, I've done nothing but cause you trouble. I'm sorry." Tears welled up in her eyes and trickled down her pale cheeks. "I'm so sorry."

"Stop it. If you apologize again, I won't be responsible for my actions." There was a kind of gentle anger underlying the words.

Brittany gasped, gripping his arm, her nails digging into his skin. Michael coached her through it, casting a worried glance at the clock. The pains seemed to be getting closer together faster than they should be. When the contraction eased, she lay back, too exhausted to protest when he stripped her soaked nightgown over her head and moved to the dresser to get a dry one.

When she'd hesitantly asked if he wanted to be her labor coach, she hadn't really thought ahead to the intimacy that was going to result from the request. First there'd been the classes, where it had been assumed that they were a typical couple—how else would she have gotten in the condition she was in?

She'd gradually grown accustomed to the feel of his hands on her stomach as he followed the teacher's instructions. Only occasionally did she think of the kiss they'd shared in the kitchen, never to be repeated, never to be spoken of, never to be forgotten.

It was only now that she was realizing the extreme intimacy of the task she'd given him. He eased the fresh gown over her swollen body, making it seem the most natural thing in the world.

She lay back, drifting, hazily aware that Michael was calling her doctor, warning him that she was on her way. She roused when he brushed the hair back from her face, opening her eyes. Somehow, it wasn't possible to believe that anything could go wrong when she looked into the calm blue of his gaze.

"Come on, let's get you to the hospital." She held his arm as he lifted her gently to her feet, guiding her into her slippers and then through the living room to the front door. He dragged her coat out of the closet, directing her arms through the sleeves as if she were a child.

The next contraction hit before he could get her out the door. Michael held her, coaching her through it. He glanced at his bare wrist, wishing he'd thought to pick up his watch. He didn't know exactly how far apart the pains were, but he knew they were coming faster than he'd been told to expect. When the pain eased, he bent and scooped her into his arms, carrying her outside and down the steps.

The frosty ground crunched beneath his feet. Spring

might be only a few weeks away, but winter was in no hurry to release it's chilly grip. Brittany looped her arms around his neck, totally confident that he held her safe and sound.

The Mustang started with a roar, and Michael cranked the heater on high, though looking at Brittany, he didn't think the chilly air was high on her list of discomforts. She looked so pale and so young. For an instant, he felt a blinding flash of rage that she was going through this. How could Dan have been so bloody irresponsible?

He wasn't sure what made him madder, the fact that Dan had gotten himself killed or the fact that he'd left Brittany alone and pregnant.

He backed the Mustang out of the driveway, shifting it into gear as gently as possible, as if afraid that the smallest jolt might cause her pain. Glancing at her, he felt a stab of fear. She was lying back in the low seat, her eyes closed. She was so small. What if this delivery didn't go smoothly?

The thought haunted him all the way to the hospital. Twice on the short drive he pulled off to the side of the road, coaching Brittany through contractions. The streets were empty. At 3:00 a.m., Remembrance slept.

The doctor arrived at the hospital only minutes after Michael carried Brittany in. His calm assumption that they'd have plenty of time before the baby arrived disappeared when he examined Brittany. Contrary to medical tradition, this was one first baby who was in a hurry to make an appearance.

Michael never left Brittany's side. With each contraction that wrenched at her, new lines etched themselves beside his mouth. He felt so helpless in the face of her pain. The breathing exercises seemed a frivolous contribution as the contractions became almost continuous.

For Brittany, Michael was the only reality in a world that had become alien and full of pain. She held his forearms, feeling the strength of the muscles there. Her eyes clung to his through a haze of pain, drawing on the strength she saw there as surely as she drew on the physical strength of his arms.

Sweat dripped from Michael's forehead as he struggled to maintain the calm facade that was all he could offer. In the final, wrenching moments, Brittany dug her nails into Michael's arms drawing blood. He welcomed the pain, wanting nothing more than to be able to draw her agony into himself.

"Push, Brittany." The doctor's voice was calm, coming to her through a fog.

"I can't," she gasped. But suddenly she had to push, as if a force outside her control demanded it. Her neck arched with the effort, Michael's soothing touch the only reality. There was a moment of tremendous pressure and then a sudden relief. She sagged, panting.

"You have a beautiful little girl."

Brittany blinked, trying to clear her vision. "Is she all right?" she got out raggedly.

"She's just fine." As if to punctuate the doctor's words, a thin cry pierced the air. The doctor turned to Michael. "Would you like to introduce your wife and daughter?"

Michael held out his arms automatically, unable to drag his gaze from the squirming red bundle the doctor was handing him.

"Let me see her." Brittany struggled up, unaware of the nurse who propped pillows behind her, giving her exhausted body support.

Michael bent, laying the tiny infant in her waiting arms. Brittany laughed tearfully as she tugged aside the soft blanket, carefully counting tiny fingers and toes.

"Look at her. She's perfect," Brittany's tone was soft in deference to the miracle she held.

Michael reached out to touch one of the little fists that waved aimlessly. His heart bumped as tiny fingers closed over his finger.

"She likes her daddy already." The nurse's comfortable comment brought Michael's eyes to Brittany's. Need lodged in his throat. Her eyes never left his as she answered the nurse.

"She does seem to know him, doesn't she?"

Michael's eyes fell to the infant she held. The baby still held his finger, but, in that instant, his heart dropped into her tiny fists.

Danielle Elizabeth Sinclair was his by right of ties much stronger than shared genes.

Brittany turned her head when she heard the door of her room open, smiling at her visitor.

"Beth."

"How are you feeling?" Beth crossed the room, setting a small arrangement of baby's breath and pink rosebuds on the table next to the bed before bending to kiss Brittany's cheek.

"I'm fine. Have you seen her?"

"I stopped by the nursery on the way up. She's beautiful."

"Thank you." Brittany leaned back against the pillows, filled with a mixture of elation and lingering exhaustion.

"Donovan will be up in a minute. I left him parking the car. I think Michael has plans to collar him in the lobby and take him to see Danielle before he gets up here."

Brittany laughed. "Michael thinks she's more of a miracle than I do, I believe. He was wonderful during the delivery. I don't know how I'd have gotten through it without him."

"He called us at five-thirty this morning to give us the news. He sounded almost drunk."

"It was quite an experience," Brittany said softly.

"I know." Beth's eyes dropped but not before Brittany caught the flare of heartache in them.

"Oh Beth, I'm sorry." She reached out to touch the other woman's arm. "We never talked about it, but Michael told me about—" She stopped, wondering if she was stepping over a boundary she wasn't welcome to cross.

"About me losing the baby?" Beth finished for her.

"Yes. I wondered... I mean, I hope it wasn't too painful for you, my being pregnant and now this."

"It wasn't painful for me. Or, at least, it wasn't very often. Besides..." She hesitated as if debating whether or not to continue. Her eyes lifted to Brittany's, and she finished in a rush. "I think, maybe, I'm pregnant again."

"Oh, Beth, congratulations."

"Well, it's too soon for congratulations. I haven't even mentioned it to Donovan. I don't want him to worry. I haven't had it confirmed yet, but I'm sure."

"Everything will be fine this time. I just know it will."

"I hope so."

The conversation lagged briefly, and then Beth shook her head, forcing a wide smile. "Why are we talking about me when you've just produced a small miracle? What a selfish idiot I am.''

Brittany protested that she was nothing of the kind, but she was not adverse to changing the subject. Beth sat on the edge of the bed and listened to her talk; concern clouding her eyes. She wondered if Brittany realized how often Michael's name came up. Remembering his call this morning and the look of dazed pride in his eyes when she'd seen him at the nursery, she couldn't help but worry.

The two of them had gone into this marriage with such clear-cut plans. She didn't think either of them had given much thought to the way emotions could shift, making all their plans irrelevant. Whatever it was they felt for each other, she knew that Michael loved that baby as if it were his own. What would it do to him if Brittany was to take her and leave?

''Beth?'' Brittany's questioning tone snapped her out of her thoughts.

''What? I'm sorry. I didn't mean to drift off on you.''

''You looked so distant, as if you were a million miles away.''

''Did I? I guess I am a little.''

''Why?''

Beth smoothed a hand over her skirt, telling herself to keep out of it. It was really none of her business. Michael wouldn't welcome her interference. Still, she couldn't just stand by and see him get hurt without trying to do something to prevent it.

''Actually, I'm worried about Michael.''

''About Michael?'' Brittany's brow furrowed, her eyes darkening with apprehension. ''He seemed fine when I saw him a little while ago. What's wrong?''

"Nothing," Beth assured her hastily, already doubting the wisdom of this conversation. Donovan would have told her to keep her nose out of it. "There's nothing wrong with him."

"Then why are you worried?" Brittany asked.

"Well..." Why had she started this? Michael would be furious. "It's just that Michael seems to feel very close ties with Danielle." She spoke slowly, trying to pick her words with care. "I'm concerned about what's going to happen when you...when you and he... I'm sorry. This is none of my business. God, I'm getting to be a busybody in my old age. Forget I said anything."

Brittany reached out, catching Beth's hand when she went to stand up. "Wait. Please. I don't think you're a busybody."

"Well, I'm sure you'd be alone in that opinion," Beth said ruefully. "Michael would disown me if he knew I'd said anything, and Donovan would think I was crazy to interfere. Really, forget I said anything at all."

"Beth, I don't mind. Really, I don't. I think—I hope that we've become friends over the past few months," she said shyly. "I know I think of you as a friend."

"And I think of you as a friend." Beth's handclasp was warm. "I just don't want to see Michael hurt, that's all."

"I understand." She looked down, plucking at the bed cover, her eyes on the aimless movement. "I hadn't thought about it much. In fact, I'm realizing that there were a lot of things I didn't think about," she added ruefully. "But when Danielle was born and the doctor handed her to Michael and he gave her to me..." She shook her head, lacking the words to describe the moment. "It felt...right, as if it couldn't have been any other way, as if he really was her father. I don't know, maybe it sounds silly."

"I think it sounds beautiful."

"It was an incredible moment. I wouldn't ever want him to feel any less of a father to her. If we go our separate ways, I would still consider—like for him to— I don't want her to grow up without a father, and I can't imagine anyone who'd make a better one."

"I think that's probably the nicest compliment you could give him," Beth said, and she wondered if Brittany was aware of what her words revealed. *If* they went their separate ways?

"There she is." Michael said it as if he were presenting something so miraculous that his audience was likely to be struck down. Donovan peered through the window of the nursery, studying the sleeping child. It was clear some comment was necessary.

"She's very...small."

"Seven pounds," Michael informed him proudly, as if her weight were a significant accomplishment.

"That's great. How is Brittany?"

"Fine. The doctor said it was an easy delivery. It didn't seem like it at the time, but I guess everything did go pretty fast."

Donovan slanted a glance at his son, noticing that he hadn't taken his eyes off the sleeping child. He felt a twinge of concern at the look of adoration on his face.

"I'm glad everything went smoothly."

"It was quite an experience." Michael's smile was reminiscent. "You know, you hear so much about the miracle of birth, but it isn't really real until you actually see it happen. When they put her in my hands—" He broke off, laughing self-consciously. "I probably sound like an idiot, like I'm the first father in the world."

Donovan winced. "It is an incredible experience." He stopped, wondering if he should say anything more. But someone had to say something. "Look, Michael, it's none of my business and I know this is probably a stupid thing to say, but don't get so caught up in this that you lose sight of reality."

Michael didn't take his eyes from the baby, but his mouth tightened. "You mean the fact that she's not my child?"

Seeing the pleasure fade from Michael's face, Donovan half regretted saying anything, but it had to be said. "When you went into this marriage, it was only supposed to be temporary," he reminded. "Just until Brittany had the baby and got back on her feet. Well, she's had the baby. How are you going to feel if she takes that child and leaves?"

Michael's hand, resting on the ledge in front of the window, clenched, giving Donovan the answer even before he spoke.

"When they put her into my arms this morning, it was an experience I can't describe. It was like she filled something in me, an empty place I hadn't even known existed. I know that Dan was her father, but I was the one who was there. I was the one who felt her move for the first time and I was the first one to hold her, even before Brittany."

He shook his head, finally turning to meet his father's eyes. "She's not mine by blood, but she's mine by every other right."

"Does Brittany feel the same way?" Donovan asked quietly.

"I think so."

Donovan shook his head, looking back at the baby. "I hope you're right."

The first few weeks after Danielle's birth, Michael and Brittany were so busy concentrating on the baby that it was easy to ignore the changes occurring in their relationship. Neither mentioned the plans they'd made when they'd agreed to marry.

When Michael thought about it, he told himself that the idea had been to wait until Brittany had a chance to get on her feet again, which she certainly couldn't do while caring for a newborn. It would take time to find a job, a place to live and someone to care for Danielle while she worked.

The thought held little appeal. He didn't like the idea of someone else raising Danielle. She deserved to have her mother with her full-time. Besides, he was coming to realize just how empty the house was going to seem without the baby—without Brittany.

It was a thought he wasn't sure he wanted to examine. But he knew he didn't want to lose either of them.

Brittany smoothed her hands over her stomach, turning sideways in the mirror to check her silhouette. Not quite what it had been before she got pregnant, but not bad. It was important that she look good tonight. Michael was attending this dinner as a representative of his father's company.

The bright blue silk dress had been a present from Beth, who'd given it to her to celebrate getting her figure back. They'd grown closer these past few weeks since the baby's birth. Beth's pregnancy had been confirmed and, as she laughingly complained, Donovan had practically chained her to the house.

It seemed odd to think that, when Beth's baby was born, Danielle would have an uncle or aunt who was a year younger than she was. An uncle or an aunt. Brittany's hands shook as she smoothed the dress again, no longer seeing her reflection.

It was so easy to think of Michael as Danielle's real father. He *was* her real father in every sense but blood. He changed diapers and mixed formula as easily as she did. And Danielle responded to the sound of his voice as readily as she did to her mother's.

Sometimes it frightened her that she so rarely thought of Dan. She'd thought that the birth of the baby might bring him closer, make his memory more vivid. But it hadn't. When she looked at Danielle, she didn't think of Dan.

Was it possible that she hadn't loved him as much as she'd thought she did? Or was she just so incredibly shallow that she could let the memories go so quickly?

She reached up to touch the heart-shaped pendant Dan had given her. It seemed like decades ago now. She'd been so much younger then, so naive. So sure that life was going to work out exactly as she wanted it to.

Nothing had worked out as she'd planned. Dan had died, her parents had proved more interested in the opinions of others then they were in their daughter's welfare. She'd married a man she barely knew in order to provide a life for a child who had become the center of her life.

No, it wasn't exactly what she'd planned. But thinking about it, she realized that the only thing she regretted was Dan's death. He'd been much too young, too alive to die.

But her marriage, her daughter, even the break with her parents—those things she couldn't be sorry for. She had a healthy, beautiful child, a home. In Beth and Donovan, she'd found something of the family she'd never really had. And she had Michael.

Her fingers tightened over the pendant for a moment before dropping away.

Michael. There was the big question in her life. He was her friend, her husband in name, the person she knew she could count on. But what else?

Since Danielle's birth, they'd avoided discussing the future. But sooner or later, the future had to be faced. Their bargain had been until after the baby was born and Brittany was on her feet again. Danielle was almost two months old, and there'd been no mention of leaving.

Brittany reached for her earrings, slipping them into place with fingers that weren't quite steady. The future had to be dealt with soon, but not tonight. Tonight she was going to enjoy herself, enjoy a night out. Enjoy being Michael's wife.

# Chapter Nine

"And so, in conclusion, I'd like to say…"

Michael shifted restlessly in his seat. This was at least the third time old Harry Labell had said "in conclusion," and yet, he'd shown no signs of concluding his speech. Glancing sideways at Brittany, he saw her straighten her shoulders and open her eyes wide as if trying to stay awake. She looked as bored as he felt.

Half the room was dozing, and the other half looked as though they wished they were, too. The dinner had been even worse than the usual run of business dinners. The food had been served late and cold, but he didn't think it would have helped if it had been on time and hot. It might have been edible in a former life, but that life had probably been three or four days ago.

He'd pushed the mystery meat that had been smothered in secret sauce around his plate, while Brittany had taken two or three polite bites and then tried to look as if she were just too full to finish. An hour and three speeches later, his stomach was beginning to wonder if his throat had been cut.

On an impulse, he leaned forward and spoke in Brittany's ear.

"Are you hungry?"

"Starved," she whispered back. "But I think there're two more awards to be given."

"Are you getting one of them?"

She cast him a startled look. "Of course not. I'm not an architect."

"Well, I am and I'm not getting one, either. Let's get out of here."

"We can't. I thought this was important."

"We've made an appearance. I think that's enough. Come on, the door is just behind us. We can slip out discreetly and go get a hamburger somewhere."

"Do you think we should?"

"If we don't get out of here soon, I'm going to create a scene by eating the centerpiece," he promised her.

Brittany put a hand over her mouth to stifle the giggle that threatened to escape. "I think it's plastic."

"I don't care. It looks better than the meal did. Let's go."

He pushed back his chair, reaching for the shawl she'd draped over the back of hers. Brittany stood up, aware of eyes turning in their direction. Was it her imagination or was there real envy in some of the glances they were receiving? She followed Michael to the door, walking on tiptoes to avoid the click of heels on the hard floor.

"I'd just like to add..."

The door shut before they could hear what it was Harry planned on adding.

"They should erect a statue to that man," Michael said, "and they can put him in it."

Brittany laughed. "He is a little dull, isn't he?"

"Duller that dishwater. He's even worse face-to-face." Michael gave an exaggerated shudder. "If Dad had told me that Harry was going to be speaking, I'd have flat refused to cover for him at this thing. No wonder he stayed home. It has nothing to do with making sure Mom doesn't strain herself. He just didn't want her bored to death. And poisoned," he added with feeling.

"The food wasn't that bad."

"It was worse," he insisted. "It'll be a wonder if there aren't cases of ptomaine reported all over the state tomorrow."

"So, where are we going to get some real food?"

"I don't know." He peered through the doors of the Civic Center. "It's raining a little. Why don't you wait here while I bring the car around? Maybe by then one of us will think of something."

When the Mustang pulled up in front of the doors, Brittany hurried out and slid onto the seat.

"How about Joe's?" Michael asked the minute the door was shut.

"Joe's?"

"You know, that place that opened about six months ago on the west side of town. It's supposed to be an authentic recreation of a fifties diner. One of the secretaries at the office said they serve great food."

"Aren't we a little overdressed for that?" She looked from his dinner jacket to her silk skirt, but Michael shrugged.

"So, let's slum it a little. Right now, an enormous hamburger with a side order of chili fries sounds incredible."

Brittany's stomach chose that moment to growl. She

pressed a hand to it, giving Michael an embarrassed smile. "I guess that's your answer."

Neither of them was old enough to say for certain whether Joe's was authentic. But there was no denying the appeal of the red vinyl booths, black-and-white tile floor and waitresses dressed in poodle skirts and ankle socks.

The jukebox was just a shade too loud, blasting out Elvis and Buddy Holly, but it only added to the atmosphere. Since they'd lingered at the Civic Center until after the normal dinner hour, they got a table right away, though from what Michael had been told, there was frequently a wait to get a booth.

Sliding onto the vinyl seat across from Michael, Brittany suddenly felt young and carefree in a way she hadn't felt in a long time. Chuck Berry was complaining about Nadine, the waitress looked like something out of *American Graffiti*, and the food smelled wonderful.

Michael ordered for them. Since Danielle's birth, Brittany had been watching her diet religiously, but she didn't protest when he asked for hamburgers, chili fries and Joe's special onion rings, as well as a milk shake for each of them. Tonight, she wasn't going to bother about things like calories.

Danielle was safely tucked away at Donovan and Beth's. Brittany was out on the town for the first time in months. She felt foolishly happy.

She waited until the waitress was gone before leaning across the Formica-topped table toward Michael. "Do you realize that this is the first time we've been out together on something remotely resembling a date?"

Michael stared at her, a slow smile lighting his eyes.

"So it is. And both of us married, too. How very decadent of us."

"You won't tell my husband, will you?" Brittany widened her eyes at him, and his smile deepened.

"Does he have a very bad temper?"

"Just awful. He got extremely upset because I didn't cook the roast long enough one night."

"What a beast," he commiserated. "I won't tell him if you promise not to tell my wife."

"Is she a shrew?"

"Terrible." He nodded solemnly. "I quiver in my boots every night when it comes time to go home."

"Well, I certainly won't tell her."

Their milk shakes arrived just then, and Brittany picked hers up, lifting it to bump against Michael's in a toast.

"To guilty secrets," she said.

"To Harry Labell," Michael offered. "If he hadn't been so boring, we might still be at that dinner."

The food was as good as it smelled, and they devoured every scrap of it, though afterward, Brittany swore she couldn't possibly move, she was so full. The meal finished, they were both reluctant to see the evening end. It had been a pleasant interval, like taking a break from reality.

They lingered over the rapidly melting milk shakes as if they were glasses of fine wine, talking of everything and nothing in particular. It was almost eleven o'clock when Michael looked at his watch and reluctantly suggested that they should go pick up Danielle before his folks sent out a search party.

The rain was falling harder now, and the quiet whoosh of the windshield wipers was the only sound breaking the silence in the car. Odd, how they'd had so much to say only a few minutes ago, and now they were suddenly out of words.

Brittany was vividly aware of Michael's hand on the gearshift, so close to her leg. If he moved it just a few inches to the right... She cut the thought off, drawing her wrap closer around her shoulders.

"Are you cold?" Noticing the movement, Michael reached to turn up the heater.

"Thank you." She could have explained that it wasn't the temperature that had made her feel the need to draw some protection around her. Her eyes were drawn to his hands on the wheel. She'd always loved his hands. They were so strong. An artist's hands but with the strength of a builder.

What would they feel like on her skin? She flushed at her musings. What had gotten into her tonight? Why was she suddenly thinking things like this? Or was it really all that sudden? Hadn't she been aware of Michael for a long time now?

Well, yes, but there was aware and then there was *aware*. It was one thing to notice that he was attractive, to notice that his eyes were the same blue as a summer sky, to be aware that his hair had just the faintest touch of red woven into its darkness. It was something else altogether to start wondering what his hands would feel like on her skin, how his hair would feel threading through her fingers, what he looked like naked.

"Brittany?" Startled, she realized that the car was stopped. In front of them, a train made its leisurely way across the road.

"I'm sorry. Did you say something?" She had to clear her throat to get the words out, and her voice still held a husky note.

"Nothing important. You looked like you were a million miles away."

"Did I?"

"Yeah." But his tone was absent and, stealing a look at him, she saw that his eyes held an odd expression.

"Do I have smut on my nose or something?" she asked nervously.

"No." But he didn't look away.

"Then why are you looking at me like that?"

"I was just thinking how beautiful you are." Her eyes snapped to his, her breath catching in her chest. It was hard to see his expression in the shadowy darkness of the car, but she didn't need light to read what was in his eyes.

She didn't move, didn't blink when his hand lifted. His fingertips caressed her cheek. She couldn't take her eyes from his, couldn't breathe, couldn't think.

Her lashes drifted shut as he leaned toward her. At the first touch of his mouth on hers, she felt a deep upwelling of feeling. He'd kissed her before, but it hadn't been like this. The last time, she'd been confused, uncertain, torn between guilt and desire. Not even sure what it was she was feeling.

This time, she knew exactly what she was feeling. Desire, plain and simple.

Michael's fingers lingered against her cheek, and Brittany's hand came up to grasp his wrist as his tongue traced the line of her lips, coaxing her to open her mouth for him. Her lips parted, her fingers tightening around his wrist as his tongue explored the soft invitation of her.

He tasted of hunger. There was a promise of something warm and exciting in the feel of his mouth, the feel of his hand on her cheek. Passion.

She moaned softly, her head tilting back in a surrender as old as time. Michael's mouth hardened over hers, deepening the kiss, letting her taste his desire.

Brittany forgot where they were, forgot the tangled history that lay between them, forgot everything but the feel of Michael's kiss.

The raucous blast of a horn behind them shattered the fragile web of the moment. Still, it wasn't possible to break away too quickly. Brittany opened her eyes, feeling as if her lashes were much too heavy. Michael's eyes were locked on hers, their expression unreadable. For a moment, she felt as if he were about to say something.

The horn sounded impatiently behind them, and Michael turned away, reaching for the gearshift. The train was gone, the barriers lifted. Brittany shifted in her seat, staring through the windshield at the rainy night as the car bumped over the tracks. Except for the slap-slap of the wipers and the low growl of the engine, there wasn't a sound in the car.

Surely one of them should say something. Hadn't everything just changed? They'd just tossed all the rules out the window. This wasn't like the other kisses. This time, there was no baby to remind them of their reasons for marrying. This time, if there'd been no interruption, if they'd been at home instead of where they were, she wasn't sure it would have stopped with a kiss.

Brittany shivered. She'd wanted Michael. If they'd been somewhere private, if Michael had taken it a step further, would she have gone along? Would she have slept with him, made love with him? She closed her eyes on the realization that the answer was yes.

She didn't love him, at least not the way she'd loved Dan, but she would have made love with him. Her skin tingled at the thought of him touching her intimately, holding her, making love to her. She flushed, her eyes snapping open. Sleeping with Dan had gone against everything she'd been taught, but she'd loved him.

How could she feel this way about Michael when she'd buried her heart with Dan? How could she forget him so easily? Seeking comfort, she reached up to grasp the pendant Dan had given her.

Michael glanced at her, noticing the gesture, and his hands tightened on the wheel until the knuckles showed white, his jaw hardening. He had to restrain the urge to reach over and rip that damned necklace off her throat. He was coming to hate everything it represented.

*Dan was your best friend.*

But he was dead. He was dead and nothing in the world could change that. Brittany was *his* wife, not Dan's.

*In name only.*

The reminder didn't improve his mood. Tonight, that could have changed. If circumstances had been different...

*If wishes were horses, beggars would ride. What makes you think she'd have you?*

She'd wanted him. He hadn't dreamed the way her mouth had softened under his. She'd practically melted. And she hadn't been thinking about Dan then. For those few minutes, she'd been all his.

He wanted her that way again. Wanted it so badly it was an ache in his gut. He should have been appalled at the jealousy he felt toward Dan, his best friend—his *dead* friend.

Not another word was spoken between them as they picked the baby up and drove home. They exchanged polite good-nights in the living room, then retired to their separate bedrooms.

Michael watched Brittany disappear into her room, Danielle in her arms. Restless, he poured himself a short Scotch. He no longer had any doubts about what he wanted. He wanted Brittany. He wanted her and the baby as a permanent part of his life.

He stared into the empty fireplace, his expression brooding. All he had to do now was convince Brittany that she wanted the same thing.

Summer arrived in a blast of heat. Spring was rushed aside to allow sweltering sunshine to bake the Indiana cornfields. Farmers watched the endless blue skies and muttered of drought. Public swimming pools were jammed with people seeking a momentary respite from the heat.

Michael and Brittany skimmed over the surface of their lives, avoiding any conflict, any discussion of the future. Those few moments of shared passion had thrown a new element into their relationship.

Brittany kept telling herself that the time had come for her to start looking for a job, looking for day care for Danielle. She should be pulling her life together so that she could leave Michael to get on with the life he'd put on hold to help her.

But each day she put it off. It was too hot to drag the baby around looking at apartments and jobs. As soon as the weather broke, then she'd really knuckle down.

But the weather didn't break. It ground on, short-ening tempers as it baked the cornfields. Brittany would have liked to blame her own irritability on the weather, but honesty demanded that she admit, at least to her-self, that the heat had nothing to do with it.

Danielle was unusually fussy, protesting the extreme temperatures in the only way she could, but that wasn't what had her mother's temper on edge. Brittany didn't have to look far for the cause of her moodiness. It could be summed up in one word.

Michael.

He was so...there. He wasn't home any more than he had been. It was just that when he was home, he seemed to take on more of a presence, somehow.

She stirred restlessly against the sheets. Danielle slept peacefully in her crib, carefully placed to catch just the edge of the breeze from the window air con-ditioner Michael had installed last week when he'd re-alized how miserable the heat was making the infant.

The cool air was enough to soothe Danielle, but her mother needed something more. A rumble of thunder sounded in the distance, and Brittany swung her legs out of bed. A look at the clock told her that it was after midnight. Danielle would be awake by six. She should go to sleep. But sleep didn't seem likely.

She moved to stand in the middle of the room, di-rectly in the flow of air from the air conditioner. It felt wonderful and she opened her arms wide as if embrac-ing the breeze. It stirred her nightie, molding it to her figure like a lover's touch. Her nipples puckered in response, and she closed her eyes, letting her thoughts drift.

What if Michael was to open the door and see her standing here? Would he want her? Would his eyes darken to that stormy blue? Would he want to touch her breasts, kiss them?

She groaned, her eyes flying open. Ever since the night he'd kissed her in the car, her thoughts had shown a tendency to drift in this vein. It was as if he'd lighted a fire inside her that wouldn't go out.

It wasn't right to want a man like this. It was one thing to love a man, and a natural outgrowth of that love was physical desire. But she didn't love Michael. She cared about him, cared a great deal. And maybe in a way she loved him. But she didn't *love* him. Not the way she'd loved Dan. She had loved Dan. Hadn't she?

Shocked that she could even ask that question, she turned, catching a glimpse of herself in the mirror. A ghostly figure in white, with no more substance than a spirit. That was how she felt, as if she'd been drifting through her life, letting events push her here and there, never really taking control.

She turned away from the reflection, suddenly feeling as if she were suffocating. The room was too small. She fled, aware that she was running away from her own thoughts more than anything else.

Despite the hour, the heat lingered in the rest of the house. Michael had left the windows open, and a breeze drifted through, giving at least the illusion of cooler temperatures. Was it her imagination, or was there a hint of dampness in that breeze? Thunder rumbled again as she moved to a window, looking out over the broad sweep of flat land behind the house. Far off, into the distance, she could see a flash that might have been lightning, but it was impossible to be sure.

Lifting her hair with her hands, she closed her eyes, turning her face to the breeze. Restlessness gnawed at her. She wanted. She couldn't define what it was, but there was an aching hunger inside that had to be assuaged.

"Looks like we might get some rain."

The quiet comment made her spin around, and she put a hand against the window frame to catch her balance. Michael stood there, his face in shadow. Brittany's eyes caught the muscles of his bare chest, the dark hair that dusted across it before narrowing into a fine line that ran over his taut stomach and disappeared into the waistband of his unsnapped jeans.

Sheer force of will dragged her eyes upward to his face. Michael lifted the glass he held, ice tinkling as he sipped the Scotch.

"What do you think?"

"'Think'?" Her voice came out too high, and she cleared her throat, trying again in a more normal tone. "Think about what?"

"Do you think we're going to get some rain?" He took a step closer to look out the window, and Brittany closed her eyes for an instant, feeling almost dizzy. He was so close. Too close. Not close enough.

"I...don't know. Maybe. This heat wave has got to break sooner or later."

"So the weather bureau keeps saying." He let his eyes settle on her again, but his expression was hooded, impossible to read. "Is your room cool enough?"

"Yes. Danielle is sleeping like a baby." She giggled, putting her hand to her throat. "I suppose she would have to sleep like a baby, wouldn't she?"

She was babbling like an idiot. Why was she so nervous all of a sudden? This was Michael. Steady, dependable Michael. So he'd kissed her once or twice; so she'd sometimes caught him watching her with an expression she didn't understand. That was no reason to be nervous.

"I'm surprised you aren't in there, where it's comfortable," he commented, lifting the glass again.

"I couldn't sleep." She shrugged, trying not to notice the width of his chest. "I felt restless."

"So did I."

"Really? Well, this heat is enough to make anybody restless." She cleared her throat, aware that he hadn't taken his eyes off her face. "I guess I ought to get back to bed."

"Are you hot, Brittany?"

Had he moved closer or did it just seem that way? And why did that question seem to have a double meaning?

"I...it is rather warm in here, isn't it?"

"You look cool in that nightgown," he told her.

"Do I? Well, I guess it's about as cool as you can get. Except maybe being naked."

She bit her tongue, wishing she could take the last word back. Now was not the time to be mentioning things like being naked. Not even when all she could think about was what it might feel like to be naked with Michael.

Thunder rumbled again, sounding closer this time. She should move, should go back to her room and shut the door, lock out the madness she could feel stirring inside. She'd be safe there, safe from what she was feeling, what she wanted to feel.

She gasped when Michael reached out, gently pressing the icy glass just above the scooped neckline of her nightie, the shock against her skin creating a white-hot sensation.

"I could help you cool off," he whispered, his voice husky.

"I don't think cooling off is what would happen—" She broke off, biting her lip against a moan as he let the glass slide lower until it pressed against her nipple through the fine batiste.

"Do you want to cool off?" He moved the glass back and forth in tiny stroking movements, dampening the fabric with the condensation on the glass.

Brittany reached behind her, her fingers clenching over the windowsill. This wasn't what she'd planned.

*Wasn't it? Then why did you come out here half-dressed?*

"Do you really want to cool off?" He moved closer, subtly trapping her. The glass moved to the other nipple, and this time she couldn't bite back the tiny moan. "You don't sound like you're ready to cool off," he murmured. "You sound hot. As hot as I feel."

Her back to the window, she couldn't move when he stepped closer, his free hand settling on her hip, drawing her forward until their thighs were touching. She could feel him through the fabric of his jeans, pressing against her.

"Tell me what you want, Brittany."

Odd, how the cold glass could start a fire in the pit of her stomach.

"Tell me." He pressed closer, letting her feel how much he wanted her.

A breeze swirled through the window, catching the fabric of her nightie and blowing it forward so that it wrapped around Michael's hips, binding them together.

"Please." The one word was all she could get out. It was enough. The heavy glass thudded to the floor. One hand flattened against her back, jerking her forward until she lay on the warm skin of his chest. The other wrapped itself in her hair, anchoring her for his kiss.

At the first touch of his body, Brittany felt as if something had broken loose inside. Months of pent-up passion were in that kiss. How long had she wanted him? Since that kiss in the car? Since the wedding? Since the first moment she'd met him? How could she not want him?

Her hands were shaking as she ran them over his chest, feeling the hard muscles there. His tongue thrust deep, engaging hers in erotic love play. His hand slid down her back to her thighs, finding the hem of her nightie and inching it upward. Cupping her buttock, he drew her up so that she could feel his aching need against the very heart of her.

She moaned, her head falling back, hair streaming down her spine. Michael began to explore the length of her throat, leaving soft, moist kisses at every interval. She shared his frustration when the neckline of her gown blocked his path. His hand left her hair, and she laughed shakily at the sharp sound of ripping cotton.

He cupped her breast, the callused surface of his palm abrading the delicate skin. She sighed, her fingers coming up to lock in his hair when his mouth closed over her at last. The feel of his tongue and teeth on her nipple was something she'd dreamed of. Dark, secret dreams she hadn't admitted to—not even to herself.

She felt the tugging at her breast and felt it deep inside, a visceral drawing that she wouldn't—couldn't—deny. She drew him closer, arching her back to offer herself to him.

Outside, lightning flashed, unmistakable now as the storm swept across the prairies. The boom of thunder was barely heard over the pounding of two hearts, the soft moans of pleasure.

Michael moved his attentions to her other breast. Brittany lowered her hands, suddenly impatient with the remaining barriers between them. The zipper of his jeans rasped in the still air, and then her hand slid inside, cupping him. He shuddered and she felt a surge of purely feminine power that this man trembled at her touch.

He dragged away from her breast, catching her mouth with his. His hand moved between her thighs, finding her damp invitation. Brittany trembled, her moan lost in his mouth. If she hadn't been pinned between Michael's broad frame and the window, she would surely have sunk to the floor, her knees unable to support her.

Michael pulled his mouth from hers, his chest heaving with the effort he was making. "I don't think I can wait. I want you so much."

"I don't want to wait. I want you now." Later, she'd wonder if that wanton invitation could really have come from her.

Michael groaned, reaching to rid himself of his jeans and stripping the ruined nightie from her willing body before he lowered them both to the floor. The carpet was soft against her back, but she wouldn't have noticed if it had been rock-covered ground. All that mattered was the man poised above her.

Lightning flashed, illuminating him in silhouette as he nudged her knees apart, settling against her. Thunder cracked, drowning her cry of pleasure as he thrust deep.

It was everything she'd ever fantasized and more. He filled her, surrounded her, made her whole. Nothing had ever felt like this; nothing could ever feel like this again.

There was a rush of sound as the storm reached them. The clouds opened, pouring rain onto the thirsty earth. Moisture blew through the open window, dampening the taught muscles of Michael's back. Brittany's fingers slipped on his tanned skin, as she sought something to cling to in a world that spun crazily around her.

The emptiness was filled. Not just the physical emptiness, but a deeper, aching hollow she refused to acknowledge. It was as if a part of her had been missing and was now found in Michael's arms.

Thunder cracked, the sound so close it rocked the house. But the storm outside paled in comparison to the storm that was raging inside. Every movement, every touch sent the tension inside her spiraling higher until Brittany thought she would surely explode. But it was the world around her that dissolved into a million pieces, leaving her floating on a sea of pleasure so intense, she could hardly breathe.

Michael's mouth caught her cry of fulfillment, his body arching heavily against hers as he followed her into the wildly spinning glory.

It was a long time before Brittany returned to earth. The thunder and lightning had moved on, leaving the rain behind. She was aware of the cool dampness that blew in through the window, vaguely aware that the carpet was probably getting ruined. But the only important thing was Michael's solid weight over her. She murmured a protest when he lifted himself.

"I'm not going anywhere," he told her, his voice husky. She caught the gleam of his teeth as he flashed a smile. "How dumb do you think I am?"

He sank down beside her, stroking his hand along her side. She stretched, feeling like a particularly well-fed cat. Michael's palm covered her breast, surprising a whimper of pleasure from her. Her eyes flashed wide as his fingers caught a tender nipple, tugging it gently. She'd never have believed that passion could be roused so quickly after what they'd just shared. But his touch brought a familiar tightness to her lower stomach.

His knee wedged between her thighs as his head bent, his teeth catching one taut bud.

"You aren't tired, are you?"

"No," she managed breathlessly, feeling every nerve come to quivering life. "I'm not tired."

"Good. Because neither am I."

He twisted, drawing her over him, and Brittany gave herself up to the pleasure he sent pulsing through her.

# Chapter Ten

It was still dark when Michael woke, though the darkness was faintly gray around the edges, as if to show that dawn wasn't far away. The rain that had started with a bang now fell gently on the parched fields. Somewhere in the distance, he could hear the muffled rumble of thunder.

Brittany slept beside him, her body curled confidingly close. Her hair spilled across his chest like a silky black web. Even though the scent of their lovemaking lingered in the air, he tried desperately to ignore his body's response to the musky smell.

He eased his arm out from under her head. She stirred but didn't wake, cuddling up to the pillow in a way that made him want to kiss her awake. But he needed to think.

He picked up his jeans on the way out of the room, thrusting his legs into them in the hallway. He eased open Brittany's door and padded quietly over to the crib. Danielle was awake, and she stared up at him solemnly, as if asking why it had taken him so long to get here.

"Hello, sweetie. Have you been awake long? You were certainly very good to keep quiet. Mommy's still asleep, so you'll just have to muddle through with Daddy for now."

He kept up the silly patter as he changed her diaper, then he carried her into the kitchen. He held her on one hip while he got a bottle out of the refrigerator and set it to warm in the microwave. Carrying her into the living room, he settled her in a corner of the sofa with the bottle propped on a pillow while he shut the window. His toes squished in the carpet underneath, but he had other things to think about besides the possibility of a ruined carpet.

Sitting on the sofa, he lifted Danielle into his arms, holding the bottle. She watched him with wide eyes as she nursed, eyes that were changing from baby blue to a more distinct blue. Her hair was darkening, too, showing promise of being the same rich black as her mother's someday.

"You know, life's easy for you now. Enjoy it while you can, angel. It certainly does get complicated when you grow up."

He leaned his head back against the sofa, staring up at the ceiling. Outside, the rain fell steadily. The back of the heat wave had been broken, and the air felt pleasantly cool.

Everything had seemed so simple last night. When he'd seen Brittany in that sweetly sexy gown, felt the restlessness in her—a restlessness he more than understood... He shook his head, looking back down at the baby he held.

Dan's child.

That was harder and harder to remember. From the moment of her birth, she'd been his. Just as he'd come to look on Brittany as his. His wife.

Somewhere along the way, like some great cosmic joke, he'd ended up living the life Dan should have had. His wife, his baby. It all should have been Dan's. And what did that make him? Instead, he'd stolen that life and made it his own.

"Michael?" He lifted his head at Brittany's soft call. She stepped into the swath of light that spilled from the kitchen. Despite his confused state of mind, his body tightened in familiar reaction. She'd pulled on one of his shirts, and the blue cambric draped her figure in a way that revealed nothing but hinted at everything. Her hair lay in a thick black cloud on her shoulders, tousled with sleep and loving.

His hand tightened around the bottle he still held, though Danielle had long since drained it and was drifting off to sleep. How was it possible for one woman to be every fantasy he'd ever had?

"Did Danielle cry?" Brittany moved closer, a slight frown creasing her forehead, disturbed by the thought that the baby might have cried and she hadn't heard her.

"No. I went in to check on her and she was awake, so I changed her and fed her. Looks like she's just about asleep again."

"Why don't I put her to bed," Brittany suggested.

"Sure." Michael stood up, letting her take the drowsy infant from his arms. This close, he could smell the warm, womanly scent of her, and his jaw tightened against the urge to take her in his arms, bury his face in her hair.

Her eyes met his and he read the uncertainty she was

feeling. His hand half lifted and then dropped. If he touched her, he was going to take her back to bed. She looked away.

"I'll make a pot of coffee," he said, stalling for time. There was no need to discuss the fact that they had to talk. The events of the night before had rearranged all their neat plans, changed everything.

When Brittany came into the kitchen, she'd changed into a pair of jeans and a loose top, and she'd brushed her hair. But there was still a touch of color in her cheeks, a certain look in her eyes that spoke of a woman who'd been thoroughly loved. Despite his own doubts about where they went from here, Michael took a purely masculine satisfaction in that look.

"Here. I thought you might want to put this on." Brittany's eyes settled on his bare chest and then skittered away as she held out the shirt she'd been wearing earlier.

Michael half smiled as he took the shirt from her. It was obvious that she found his naked chest a distraction. The knowledge was not unpleasant. He shrugged into the shirt, buttoning it halfway before he turned and lifted a pair of coffee cups from the counter.

"The dining room?" he questioned.

"Sounds fine."

Neither of them said a word as he carried the cups into the dining room and set them on the table. The rain fell in a gentle gray curtain outside the window, muffling the dawn that struggled to sneak through the clouds.

Brittany sat down and picked up her cup, sipping at the steaming black liquid. Not that she particularly wanted coffee, but she did want something to do with her hands. Michael sat across the table from her. If she lifted her eyes from her cup, she could see a wedge of tanned flesh between the edges of his shirt.

Since their marriage, she'd seen Michael without a shirt dozens of times but never before when she had quite such an intimate knowledge of exactly what those muscles felt like beneath her fingers.

She still wasn't sure what had happened last night. The heat, the storm, Michael. Everything sort of blended together in her mind.

"We sort of skipped a few steps," Michael offered when the silence threatened to stretch too long.

"I guess we did." She knew what he meant. There should have been stages that came before last night's explosion of passion. Somehow, they'd jumped over all the hand holding and kissing and working up to sleeping together.

He twisted the coffee cup between his hands, staring down at the aimless movement.

"Look, Brittany, I feel like I should—"

"If you're going to apologize, I'm going to dump this coffee in your lap." The guilty way his eyes swept to hers told her that that was exactly what he'd been about to do. "Michael, I wasn't a victim last night."

"I didn't think you were," he protested.

"Didn't you? Then why do I have the impression that you were about to apologize?"

"I just felt that—maybe—you might have felt that you... Well, that you owed me something."

"I do owe you. I owe you a lot more than I can ever repay, but I didn't sleep with you because I owe you."

"I don't think the sleeping part of it is the problem," he murmured drily.

Brittany felt her cheeks warm. "No, I guess it isn't."

"This changes things," he said after a long pause.

"Weren't things changing before this?"

"Yes. But this changes them with a vengeance."

"In what way?"

"I can't go back to the way things have been. After last night, making love with you, I can't pretend that we're just friends who happen to be sharing a house and a marriage license. I want you too much to even try," he said bluntly.

This time the flush started at her throat and worked its way over her face. She felt a foolish flutter in her chest. It wasn't as if his words were news. Heaven knows, he'd proved how much he wanted her last night. It was just that having it laid out as he'd done was startling.

"Okay," she managed at last, trying to sound calm and collected. "I'd agree with that. There's obviously an...attraction between us."

Michael's mouth twisted as if in silent commentary at the careful way she stated things. "I think that's pretty obvious."

There was another long silence while Brittany stared at the table. The rain continued to fall, but the sun had accomplished a partial victory, and it was at least light outside.

"So, where do we go from here?" she asked when she couldn't stand the silence another second.

"Where do you want to go from here?"

"I asked you first." She gave him a quick, nervous smile that held more panic than amusement.

"Fair enough." He nodded. "It seems to me that we only have a couple of choices. Either we stay together and make this a real marriage—" He stopped, as if weighing his next words.

"Or..." Brittany prompted at last.

"Or we break the whole thing off right now."

He said it quietly, but it still struck a blow. What he meant was that she would take Danielle and move out, just as they'd planned from the beginning. Only nothing was the way it had been in the beginning. She'd come to think of this house as her home, of Donovan and Beth as part of her family, of Michael as Danielle's father. As her husband.

She looked away quickly before he could see the impact of his words. "Is that what you want? To break it off? That's what we planned, isn't it?"

"It's what we planned," he agreed slowly.

"Is it what you want?"

The seconds ticked by as she waited for his answer. If he said yes, her whole life was going to come tumbling down around her ears. And if he said no? If he said no, then she was committing herself to something she wasn't sure she was ready for.

"No, it isn't what I want."

The simple answer set off turmoil in the pit of her stomach. She wanted to take the question back, pretend last night had never happened. She wasn't ready to make this decision, to make a commitment like this.

"What do you think?"

She opened her mouth, but no sound came out. She was at a loss for words to try to express her thoughts. She didn't even know what she was thinking, what she was feeling. How could she possibly give him an answer?

"Is it that difficult to answer?" The question brought her eyes to his face. He was looking at her, one brow raised slightly quizzically. The lightness of his tone eased some of her tension. He made everything seem a little less earth-shattering, a little less frightening.

"Yes. I mean, no." She raised her hands. "I don't know."

"That's what I've always appreciated in you—your absolute decisiveness. Your ability to make snap decisions without a moment's hesitation."

Brittany shook her head, laughing softly at his blatant teasing, but the fingers she wrapped around her coffee cup were shaky.

"I know I sound like an idiot, but I wasn't really prepared for this. I mean, until last night, everything was so simple."

"Not really." Michael leaned back in his chair. "We couldn't have gone on like that forever. I think you knew it as well as I. Something had to give, sooner or later."

"I suppose," she said.

"Look, I'm not going to pressure you. This decision is important to our future—yours, mine and Danielle's. But I'd just like to point out that we've muddled along pretty well together so far. In a couple of months, we'll have been married a year. I don't think we've done too badly."

"No, we haven't."

"Would it be so difficult to start thinking of this as a permanent arrangement?"

If she was honest, she'd admit that it wouldn't be difficult at all. Hadn't that been in her mind for the past few weeks? Why was she so nervous? They'd already built a life together.

"No." The word came out a whisper, and she cleared her throat. "No, it wouldn't be hard to start thinking of this as a permanent arrangement." She lifted her eyes to his face and brought the next words out in a rush. "Michael, are you sure you're doing this because you want to? You're not doing it because you think I can't take care of myself? Or because you don't want to lose Danielle?

"Because you've got to know that, no matter what happens between the two of us, I would never try to keep you away from her. You are her father in the truest sense of the word. I mean that.

"But I wouldn't want to try to make this a real marriage if we weren't doing it for the right reasons. We should do it because we care for each other. And because we think we could be happy together..." Brittany trailed off, aware that she'd been on the verge of babbling hysterically.

"I agree. I don't think you're helpless. And I know you wouldn't try to keep me away from Danielle, for which I thank you." He reached across the table, catching her hand in his. "Brittany, the only reason I want you to stay is because I think we could make a good marriage. I think we could be happy. I...care about you. I want to be with you."

"I care about you, too." She looked at their linked hands, and suddenly the answer seemed so simple. Why was she so panicky? This was Michael, who'd been there for her from the start. They already *had* a marriage, in all the most important senses. What difference would it make if she verbalized the commitment she already felt?

"Yes. Yes, I think I'd like to make this a real marriage."

Michael's hand tightened convulsively over hers and then relaxed. "Good." He stopped and cleared his throat. "Good."

He was nervous, she thought. The realization made her relax. He always seemed so sure, so self-confident, as if he knew exactly where he was going and never doubted that he was going to get there. But he hadn't been sure of her answer. And it had been important to him.

"Well," she said, feeling as nervous and giddy as a teenager.

"Well." Michael didn't seem to have anything to add, but his smile was wide.

"I feel like we should do something to mark the occasion."

"We've already got a marriage license. Maybe we should seal this with a kiss." The look in his eyes made her flush, but she didn't resist when his hand tugged hers, urging her out of her seat. She came around the table slowly, her fingers still in his. After last night, it was a little foolish to feel shy with him. But then, last night they hadn't just made commitments to each other.

She stopped in front of him, not quite meeting his eyes, feeling like a new bride, which, in a sense, she was. She gasped when his free arm came up to catch her around the waist, tumbling her down into his lap. Tossing her hair out of her eyes, she looked at him, meeting the teasing laughter in his look.

"I just thought we should start this marriage off on the right foot."

"You mean on the right lap?"

"I mean in the right way," he said softly, reaching up to stroke the hair back from her face. "We can make this work, Brittany. I know we can."

As she melted into his kiss, she hoped they weren't making a big mistake.


Brittany adjusted a ruffle on Danielle's lemon-yellow romper with a nervous twitch.

"Okay, when Daddy comes in, I want you to give him a big smile. Tonight is special."

Danielle stared at her, greeting this announcement with the same solemn attention she gave most comments. Looking at her, Brittany felt a surge of love. It seemed incredible that this tiny, perfect human being was really here, really hers.

At the sound of the Mustang pulling into the driveway, she straightened quickly, smoothing a hand over her hips to make sure the slim skirt of her dress was lying properly. It was silly to be so nervous, but in a sense, this was a new beginning. From now on, her marriage was much more than a piece of paper.

She'd spent the day moving her things into Michael's room. One minute she'd been sure that she was making a terrible mistake, the next sure that this was the best decision she'd ever make. By late afternoon, the seesaw of emotions had left her almost dizzy.

A long, hot bath had served to relax some of the nervous tension. She'd taken time with her makeup and pulled her hair up in a soft Gibson girl pouf, leaving a few tendrils free to caress the nape of her neck. The dress was one she'd bought more than a year ago, hoping for a special occasion that justified wearing it.

At the time she'd assumed that special occasion would include Dan. Her hand had lingered on the dress uncertainly. Things had changed so much. The dress had languished in the back of her closet, serving as a reminder of dreams unfulfilled. Tonight it could serve to celebrate the beginning of new dreams.

After she'd pulled the slim turquoise silk over her head, she'd smoothed it into place, turning sideways to make sure there were no odd bulges. All her hard work in the gym after Danielle's birth had paid off, and the silk revealed nothing she had to be ashamed of. The square-cut bodice and tiny sleeves showed just enough skin to be intriguing. Maybe it was a little fancy for dinner at home, but she wanted to show Michael that this new beginning was important to her.

Now she twisted the slim diamond bracelet on her wrist, suddenly sure that she had overdone things. Especially since, with all the time she'd spent preparing herself, she'd had very little time to worry about dinner.

Hearing Michael's footsteps on the porch, Brittany put her hand to her throat, panic all but choking her. It wasn't as if she didn't know him. After last night, they were certainly intimately acquainted. And it wasn't that she was doubting the decision to turn their marriage into something real and lasting. It was just that she was standing on the brink of a major change.

The door opened and Michael stepped into the hallway. Brittany was standing at the end of the breakfast bar that divided kitchen and dining room, one hand resting casually on the maple surface of the bar, the other clenched at her side. Michael saw her as the door shut behind him, and the smile he gave her drained most of the tension.

This was Michael. Michael, who'd become her best friend. There was nothing to be afraid of. He wasn't suddenly going to change just because they'd decided to change the terms of their bargain.

Her smile was bright with relief. She lifted her face as he crossed the distance between them. His kiss was brief but thorough, and she rested her forehead against his chest for a moment before he drew back. It seemed incredible that they'd lived together all these months, and she was just now discovering that he could melt her knees with one kiss.

He took her hands as he stepped back, holding her arms out so that he could study her.

"You look fantastic."

"Thank you." Brittany flushed at the look of blatant male appreciation he was giving her. That look set off little tingles in the pit of her stomach.

"Are we celebrating?" He glanced over her head at the steaks sitting on the counter.

"Kind of. Well, not exactly."

"There you go again, being decisive. What are we 'kind of, not exactly' celebrating?"

She laughed at his teasing, feeling the last of the nervous tension drain away.

"I thought it might be nice to mark the beginning of our marriage, the real beginning, this time. I mean, if we're going to do this, we should do it properly. Don't you think?"

"Sure. Sounds like a great idea. I wish I'd thought of it myself. How's my best girl?" He bent over Danielle, lifting her into his arms. She smiled, showing her delight in his presence as he cooed over her, telling her how beautiful she was.

Brittany watched, trying to ignore the tiny twinge of irritation she felt. She hadn't expected Michael to look at this quite the same way she did. After all, he was a man and men were notoriously insensitive when it came to things like anniversaries and celebrating new beginnings. Still, it did seem as though this were something significant enough that even a man might have taken note of it.

He glanced up from the baby, catching the annoyance on her face. Something unreadable, amusement perhaps, flashed in his eyes. Surely that was amusement.

"You know, you're right. This really is a new beginning. I think we should go out to celebrate, unless you're particularly crazy to have dinner here? You look much too pretty to be spending time in the kitchen."

"It's Friday night. We probably won't be able to get in anywhere." She was not in a cooperative mood. Saying she looked pretty wasn't enough. She wanted him to share her feelings about the significance of the step they'd taken.

"We can give it a try," Michael suggested. "We can always come home and eat steak if we can't find a restaurant. Why don't you give me a few minutes to shower and change, and then we'll see what we can do."

He didn't give her a chance to argue, thrusting Danielle into her arms and loping off to the bedroom. Brittany stared after him, aware that her lower lip was poked out in something perilously close to a pout.

"Insensitive clod," she muttered. Danielle waved her fists and made an unintelligible comment of her own.

Michael stepped out of the shower and toweled off, trying to school the grin from his face. Brittany had looked so annoyed. He probably shouldn't tease her, but he found it hard to resist.

Stepping into the bedroom, he opened the closet and reached for a shirt, only to come up with a handful of silk. She'd moved her clothes into his room. He stared at the slightly overcrowded closet, feeling an odd tightness in his chest. Strange, how something as small as seeing her dresses hanging next to his shirts should seem so significant.

He pulled a shirt and a pair of slacks from the closet and shut the door, his expression thoughtful. He dressed and combed his hair, shrugging into a linen sport jacket before reaching for the small box he'd tucked into his back pocket before coming into the house.

He didn't open the box. He knew what it contained. Maybe this hadn't been such a good idea. Maybe he should wait awhile before giving it to her. His jaw set stubbornly. If they were going to make a new start, they might as well make a clean sweep. He thrust the box into the pocket of his jacket before leaving the bedroom.

Brittany said very little as they got in the car, settling Danielle into her car seat. She was still a trifle disgruntled that Michael seemed to be taking this whole thing so casually. Though, glancing at his profile, she wondered if that was really the case. He looked rather stern, as if he had something on his mind.

Her first clue that things weren't quite what she'd thought was when Michael took the turn to his parents' home.

Catching her questioning glance, he shrugged.

"I thought we'd drop Danielle off with my folks so we could have the evening to ourselves."

"Don't you think we should have called first, to make sure your mother is up to it?"

"I'm sure she won't mind. She and Dad both love having Danielle around." He stopped in front of the house and reached for the buckle on the baby's car seat. "I'll take her up," he said hastily when Brittany moved to get out of the car. "There's no sense in you getting your feet wet."

Since the sun had been out since early afternoon, and there was a walkway all the way to the front door, Brittany couldn't see how she was going to get her feet wet by getting out of the car. But something in Michael's tone made her acquiesce, and she settled back into her seat, watching as he carried the baby up to the door, diaper bag slung over one shoulder. The door opened and he handed Danielle over to Donovan, who held her comfortably in the crook of one arm. The transfer was so prompt and smooth, it was almost as if it had been arranged ahead of time. But Michael had suggested going out on the spur of the moment. Hadn't he?

She studied his face surreptitiously as he got back in the car. There was something there she couldn't quite define.... Excitement? As though maybe he knew something she didn't know? As though maybe this dinner out hadn't been quite so spontaneous as it had seemed?

She snuggled back into her seat, feeling suddenly much better.

Brittany was hardly surprised when he pulled the car to a halt in front of Chez Coeur, Remembrance's one and only French restaurant. It also happened to be the fanciest restaurant in town, with a reputation for fine food, superb service and prices that compensated for both. High prices or no, she knew they pulled their clientele from as far away as Indianapolis.

A bubble of excitement threatened to explode in a smile. Michael would never have brought her here unless he had reservations. And, if he had reservations, then he'd planned this long before he'd gotten home and found her dressed up. Which meant that this new beginning was just as important to him as it was to her.

But she kept her expression still, allowing just a hint of pout to show. If he wanted to spring this on her as if it had just occurred to him, then she wasn't going to spoil his fun.

She didn't have to maintain the facade of indifference for long. The moment they walked in the door, it was obvious that they were expected. The maître d' greeted Michael by name, his smile ingratiating enough to indicate that he'd been very well tipped ahead of time. They were shown to a table in a dimly lighted corner and seated with a flourish.

Once alone, Brittany looked across the table, raising her eyebrows at Michael. "Why don't we just see if we can get in someplace?" she questioned.

"I wanted it to be a surprise. And I managed to pull it off, didn't I?" He grinned at her, looking pleased with himself.

"I actually called you an insensitive clod in front of Danielle. I could have marked her for life."

"Well, I'm sure when you explain to her that I'm really a rather wonderful guy, she'll understand."

The evening seemed blessed. The atmosphere was quietly elegant. The service was prompt and nearly invisible, a perfect combination. And the food was superb. Brittany knew it was superb because it couldn't have been anything less, but she couldn't have said just what it was she ate.

The conversation was intermittent, but the occasional silences were comfortable. For the first time, they spoke of the future, because for the first time, they had a future together.

Michael told her of his plans for his career, his

hopes, his aspirations. And Brittany told him that she'd always dreamed of being a writer, how she'd wanted to major in journalism but her parents had insisted on a more practical degree.

It wasn't until the meal was over and they were lingering over coffee so smooth it practically evaporated on the tongue, that Michael sprang his final surprise.

"I bought you something to celebrate our marriage."

Brittany glanced up from her cup, her eyes showing her surprise as he set a small flat box on the table.

"You didn't have to do that."

"I know I didn't *have* to. I wanted to." He fiddled with the box, sliding it back and forth on the thick linen tablecloth. "I wasn't sure what you'd like."

"I'm sure I'll love it." There was a pause, but he made no move to hand her the box. She had the odd impression that he was uncertain now that the moment had come, and her curiosity inched up a notch.

After a long moment where he continued to toy with the box, he suddenly pushed it across the table to her.

"Maybe I should have gotten something else," he muttered as much to himself as to her.

Brittany took the box, trying to imagine what on earth he could have gotten her that would inspire such doubts. She peeled the wrapping away to reveal a small jeweler's box bearing the same name as the one that had held her bracelet. Snapping open the lid, she was stunned to see an exquisite diamond pendant lying on the dark velvet background. The stone caught the light, refracting it back in a hundred rainbow patterns.

"Michael, it's beautiful." She tore her gaze away from the pendant and looked at him, her eyes shining with excitement. The look of brooding uncertainty didn't leave his eyes when he smiled.

"I wanted you to have something really special to remember this night by. The night that we are truly starting our marriage."

"I certainly won't be able to forget it with something like this to remind me. I can't belive you thought I might not like this. Would you help me put it on?"

He moved around the table to the chair next to hers, but he didn't immediately reach for the necklace she was holding out.

"You'll have to take off the one you're wearing," he said quietly, his eyes searching hers.

It was suddenly clear why he'd had his doubts about the gift. Brittany's smile faded, the hand holding the diamond sinking to the table while the other reached up to grasp the simple gold heart she'd worn almost constantly since Dan gave it to her more than a year ago.

Michael saw the realization come into her eyes, and he felt a hard knot settle in his chest. He hadn't gone into the jewelry store planning on buying her something to replace the locket. He'd simply wanted something to commemorate the occasion, just as he'd told her.

But when he'd seen the necklaces, he'd suddenly flashed back to the night before. Brittany boldly straddling his thighs, her head thrown back with the pleasure of their joining, her hair streaming down her back until it almost touched his thighs. In a flash of light, she'd been revealed—woman personified. She'd been every fantasy, every dream he'd ever had. His. His wife, his lover.

And there was the dull gleam of the golden heart hanging between her breasts.

In that instant, he'd felt a flash of rage like nothing he'd ever known before. That she was wearing something given to her by another man was a reminder that she hadn't always been his, might never belong to him completely. He'd wanted to snap the chain and throw the necklace to the ends of the earth.

Instead, he'd grasped her hips, holding her still for the rhythm he set, not satisfied until she was crying out *his name* in her pleasure. Until he was sure that, at that moment, *he* was the only man on her mind.

It had all come back to him when he saw the necklaces. Before he could think about it and decide whether or not it was really a wise move, he'd picked out the diamond Brittany now held, paying far more than was wise, determined that she wouldn't spend another night in his bed wearing the locket.

It was only later that he'd begun to wonder if he had the right to feel as he did. It wasn't as if they were going into this with stars in their eyes. Did he have the right to ask her to set aside something that linked her to Dan? But some stubborn core of him insisted that she was *his* wife, sharing *his* bed.

Now, in Brittany's eyes, he saw that she understood exactly what he was asking. This was not a gift without strings. Her fingers clung to the locket as if to a safety line.

*Fool*, he castigated himself. *She isn't ready for this. You had no right. You've blown everything with your stupid, macho pride.*

"Look, it was a stupid idea. I shouldn't have bought it. We can return the necklace, and you can pick something else out."

He reached for the necklace, hoping that they could just pretend this never happened. But Brittany didn't release the delicate chain, and Michael's hand dropped away. She stared at it for a long moment, as if studying the way it caught the light, but he didn't think she was even seeing the beautiful stone.

"No. No, I don't want to return it," she said slowly, as if reaching a decision as she spoke. "It's a beautiful necklace."

"We could get something else," he insisted. "A ring would probably be more appropriate, anyway."

"I don't want a ring. I'd like to keep this." The words came more strongly, and she lifted her eyes to his face. "I'd like to keep this," she repeated.

Michael felt the knot in his chest dissolve. Just as she'd known what he was doing when he gave her the necklace, he understood what she meant now. She was willing to let the past stay in the past. She was looking ahead to the future—a future spent with him.

"Are you sure?" His eyes searched hers.

"I'm sure." There was no doubt in her voice, and her hands were steady as she reached up to unlatch the locket. She set it in one hand, coiling the chain into her palm, staring down at it. "I've worn this long enough, I think." Drawing a deep breath, she closed her fingers over the locket and looked up at him. "Would you help me put your necklace on, please?"

Michael took the pendant from her, aware that his fingers weren't quite steady. Brittany turned so that her back was to him, and he reached over her shoulder to set the necklace in place. The tiny clasp balked at first but then slipped neatly together.

When she turned back to him, the diamond winked against the turquoise silk. Rainbow fires shot from it, like delicate promises. Which was just what it represented. Promises he hoped would never be broken. Promises he was going to do his damnedest to fulfill.

He bent to kiss Brittany, feeling her mouth soften under his. This was their true wedding ceremony. This was the real beginning of their lives together.

# Chapter Eleven

It was Christmas Eve, a year and a half later and Remembrance bustled with good cheer and people trying to get home to spend the holiday with their families. The snowfall had been light so far this winter, little more than a dusting of white covered the fields nearby and nestled in sheltered pockets in the town itself. But snowfall was promised before morning, so there was a good chance of waking up to a white Christmas, after all.

Hardly anyone noticed the lone man who walked down Main Street, coming from the bus station. If anyone had noticed him, they might have thought that he needed a heavier coat. The thin jacket he wore over his jeans was hardly protection against the chill in the air. They might also have noticed the limp that dragged at his step, and, if they happened to look real close, they might have realized that he wasn't as old as he looked at first glance.

But everyone was absorbed in the need to finish last-minute shopping at the one or two stores that remained open and get home to start celebrating. So the man walked down the sidewalk alone, his eyes hungry as he stared in every shop window. Occasionally, he reached out to touch a window or a winter-dormant tree, as if to assure himself that they were real.

He paused outside a café, drinking in the scent of coffee that drifted out as patrons entered or left. The Scout Café would be open until midnight, even tonight, he knew. And they'd have a few customers until then— those who had nowhere else to go, no one to be with.

But he wasn't one of those. In this place, he did have somewhere to go. So he turned away from the inviting smells, hunching his shoulders inside the jacket and turning the collar up to give some protection against the biting wind that skidded around the corner of the building and sought out every worn spot in his clothes.

He barely noticed the cold. His eyes were set on a goal as he limped away from the center of town. He could have called a taxi, gotten out of the biting cold, but he wanted to savor every icy step of the path he was on. Home. He was almost home.

The Sinclair house was brightly lit, light spilling from every window to create gleaming patterns on the patchy snow outside. Inside, the holiday was being celebrated in style. Family and friends filled the big house to the rafters. An enormous Christmas tree dominated one corner of the living room. Underneath it, an antique train circled. Earlier the train had been a source of great fascination for the gathering's youngest members.

But Danielle Sinclair and young Colin Sinclair had been dispatched to beds in the nursery upstairs as befitted their extreme youth. How the babies could sleep through the friendly noise below was hard to imagine, but when either Beth or Brittany checked on them, they were sleeping the sleep of the innocent.

Just now, Brittany wasn't thinking about her daughter. She wasn't thinking about anything beyond the warm promise of her husband's hands at her waist and the wicked gleam in his eyes.

She and Michael had been sent to the kitchen to get ice, but Michael didn't seem to have any intention of opening the refrigerator. He'd trapped her in a corner by the cupboard, claiming that there was mistletoe above her and she couldn't break tradition by denying him a kiss.

Laughing, Brittany pointed out that she didn't see any mistletoe, but he just told her to use her imagination and proceeded to kiss her quite thoroughly. She wound her arms around his neck, melting into the kiss, just as she always did. Two years of marriage hadn't dulled the response she felt each time he kissed her.

"I told you not to send the two of them for ice." Beth glanced up at her husband's muttered comment. Her eyes laughed into his, seeing the amusement he wasn't trying very hard to hide.

"It's Christmas Eve, Donovan. You can't expect people to be quite as efficient as they usually are."

"By the time they get out here with the ice, it very well may be New Year's Eve."

"Then we'll have a head start on that party."

Donovan grinned at her, slipping an arm around her waist and pulling her against his side. "You know, we could slip away from this shebang. Go upstairs and inspect the linen closet."

Beth smiled but whatever she'd planned to say died unspoken as she looked past him, her eyes falling on the new guest one of their friends had just opened the door to.

"Oh my God." The words were more a prayer than an exclamation.

"What is it?" Donovan turned, staring at the newcomer.

He didn't look much like a party goer. His jeans were too worn for fashion, his boots were frankly worn down at the heels. His shaggy blond hair looked as if it hadn't been cut in months, and there was a stubble of beard on his lean cheeks. But it wasn't his lack of sartorial splendor that made Donovan curse and start forward.

The move came too late. The kitchen door swung open, and Brittany stepped into the hallway, her cheeks flushed, her eyes bright. She was carrying a tray of glasses, her head half turned to see if Michael was bringing the ice. She caught Donovan's quick movement out of the corner of her eye and turned to see what had caused it. Her gaze settled on the scruffy stranger. As if sensing her look, he turned, too, his eyes meeting hers.

The tray dropped from her suddenly nerveless fingers. The resultant crash brought instant silence in its wake as people looked to see the cause. Brittany stared at the stranger, her hands coming up to cover the sudden pallor in her cheeks, her wide eyes disbelieving.

"Dan." The name was a whisper.

"Hello, Brit." He half smiled, his eyes uncertain. "Merry Christmas."

"Oh my God. Dan. It's really you."

The paralysis left her, and she flew across the hall, throwing herself into the arms he held out to her.

"I can't believe it! You're here. You're alive." She

was half laughing, half crying, oblivious to the people watching their reunion, to the murmurs starting up as the guests realized who the shaggy stranger must be. Oblivious to Michael standing in the kitchen doorway, his face white as he watched her embracing Dan.

After a stunned pause, Donovan and Beth acted together. As if they'd planned for just this eventuality, each moved forward, Donovan toward Dan and Brittany, Beth toward her son.

"I think a little privacy might be in order here," Donovan said. Dan drew his eyes from Brittany's face, a grin breaking through the worn lines that bracketed his mouth.

"Donovan! Sorry to cause a scene."

"Don't worry about it." Donovan put his hand on the younger man's shoulder, squeezing roughly. "But in a minute, you're going to be mobbed. Why don't we move into the den?"

"Sure, sure. Where's Michael? Is he here?" Dan's eyes skimmed the crowd, looking for his friend.

"I think he's probably waiting for you in the den." Donovan gently shepherded the two of them across the hall. No one approached, though it was obvious that they were all aware of the drama going on in their midst as they watched the three of them disappear into the den.

Michael turned as the study door opened. He noticed that Dan still held Brittany's hand. She was looking up at him as if she couldn't believe the miracle of his presence. But all of that he noticed peripherally.

"Michael! My God, you haven't changed a bit!"

"It hasn't been that long." The two men clasped hands, their grips too tight, each searching the other's face as if to reconfirm the familiar features.

"You look great! God, everybody looks great."

"Well, you look like hell," Michael told him with a grin.

"Thanks." If Dan's grin had gotten any wider, it would surely have split his face in two. "Good to see you, too."

There was an awkward little pause, and then Michael pulled Dan forward, throwing his arms around him in a rough hug.

"You'd better have a good explanation, you SOB."

Dan laughed, returning the hug before stepping back. "Don't I always have a good explanation? Remember the time I convinced the music teacher that your dog had run off with my trumpet?"

"Yeah, and she believed it until she found out I didn't have a dog."

"Well, I had her going for a while there." Dan reached for Brittany's hand.

"I think we'll leave the three of you alone. You can fill us in on the details later." Donovan took Beth's hand and pulled her out of the room, shutting the door behind them.

"Do you think that's wise?" Beth asked him, her worried eyes on the door.

"I think they've got a lot to work out, and I don't think we can help them do it."

"I suppose." But she didn't sound sure.

In the den, Dan sat down on the sofa, pulling Brittany with him, reluctant to lose contact with her for even an instant. Michael sank into a chair across from them. He still found it hard to believe that Dan was sitting here, just like old times.

"So come on, out with it. Where have you been for

the past two and a half years? And I hope this is a better explanation than 'the dog stole my trumpet.'"

"It's better, I guess. More complex, anyway."

"The search party found the plane. They said there were no survivors," Brittany told him gently.

"I know. At least, I know there were no survivors except me. I left the site of the crash before the search party arrived." He looked down, his face shadowed, and Michael was suddenly aware of the lines that creased his face. Dan looked older than his years. Older and worn.

"What happened?" Michael leaned forward, resting his elbows on his knees. "We thought you were in the plane. If I'd known you were alive..."

"I know, buddy. You'd have come looking. I knew that."

There was a moment's silence while each of them considered how different their lives would have been if Dan had been found by the search party. Michael avoided looking at Brittany, his emotions in a turmoil.

"What happened to you?" It was Brittany who broke the silence, her eyes tracing the lines in his face.

"I was in a prison, actually." Dan tried to speak lightly, but there was nothing light about the expression in his eyes. "In a stinking hellhole of a prison."

"Why?" The single question was all Brittany could manage.

"Mistaken identity?" He laughed bitterly, robbing the answer of any humor. He sighed, leaning back on the sofa, his eyes on things only he could see.

"I suppose it will be easier if I start at the beginning.... The project started out great. Everybody gathered in L.A., and we all had our equipment. Dad—" He broke off, swallowing. "Dad was like a little kid.

I don't think I ever saw him more excited. He was convinced we were going to discover some new civilization. More likely we'd have all ended up with sunburn and dysentery, but he was still excited.

"We took off on time, and the whole team was in good spirits. It was a good group. Nice people."

He stopped again and Michael knew he was thinking about the fact that those people were all dead.

"Anyway, everything was going great until we developed engine trouble. Right over miles of jungle. The pilot tried to set down in a clearing, but there wasn't really enough room. We hit hard, sort of like belly flopping into a pool. I was right next to an exit door, and the impact popped the door open. It wouldn't have done me any good except that my seat belt snapped, and I was thrown out. The plane skidded across the clearing and slammed into the side of a hill we hadn't even been able to see from the air. It blew like the biggest firecracker you've ever seen."

No one spoke for the space of several slow heartbeats. Brittany's hand tightened over Dan's, trying to imagine what it must have felt like to watch the plane explode, knowing that your father was inside. To know that everyone in it was instantly dead.

"Were you hurt?"

"A broken leg."

Dan shrugged, dismissing the injury as minor, which she supposed it must have seemed then, compared to what he'd just seen.

"Why didn't the search party find you?" Michael asked.

"That was my fault. I wasn't thinking too clearly at that point. Shock, I guess. For some reason, I decided that the only logical thing to do was to try and walk to civilization. I had this knife Dad had bought me, one of those with every tool known to man in the haft, and there was a compass in there, so I figured I could find the coast and there was bound to be a town on the coast.''

He shrugged. "Like I said, I wasn't thinking too clearly. Anyway, I found a branch I could use as a crutch, and I started walking. If I'd had an ounce of sense, I'd have stayed with the wreckage. But I didn't.

"Anyway, to make a long story short, before I found the coast, I stumbled into this little village. Turned out that they were guerrilla fighters trying to overthrow the government. I don't know why the hell they didn't shoot me on the spot, but I probably looked close enough to death that they figured I wasn't worth wasting a bullet on.

"They even patched me up, more or less. They didn't have a doctor, but they had a guy who was pretty skilled in basic medicine. He set my leg and kept me from dying of infection. By the time I was ready to travel, we'd developed a pretty friendly relationship.

"The only problem we had was that they wouldn't let me leave. They were afraid that, if I went to the capital, I might reveal their position to the government. But they were going to be moving camp soon, and they'd let me go then. Since I wouldn't know the position of their new camp, I couldn't do them any harm.''

"Couldn't they have gotten a message out? Something to let us know you were alive?''

He shook his head at Brittany's question. "We were miles away from a phone, and there was no other way to communicate with the outside world. Besides, these people were considered criminals. They didn't dare risk being seen.''

"You must have loved kicking your heels." Michael remembered Dan's impatience with delays of any sort. Once he'd made up his mind to do something, he wanted to do it now, not five minutes from now.

"Well, I was damned grateful to be alive. Besides, by then weeks had gone by. I knew I must have been given up for dead. I figured another couple of weeks wouldn't make much difference to me or the people back home. And they'd been good to me. They didn't have much, but they shared what little they did have.''

"So what happened? Why didn't you come home?" Brittany asked.

"Well, it was really a matter of bad timing. They were going to be breaking camp in a couple of days, and they'd already provided me with a map to the capital. My leg wasn't very strong, but I knew I could make it that far.

"Only, the government got there first. They hit the village hard. It was like the Fourth of July, with rockets screaming everywhere. Except people were dying all over the place." He rubbed his hand over his face as if to wipe away the memories.

"I was one of the lucky ones. Or at least that's what I thought. I wasn't even hurt. When the troops rounded up the few survivors, I started trying to explain who I was. That I was an American and not part of their little war.''

"They didn't believe you?" Michael asked.

"Well, they believed the part about me being an American. But they didn't believe the part about me being a noncombatant. I had a map to the capital in my pocket, and they were convinced that I was part of some subversive plot.''

''Didn't you demand to talk to the American ambassador or consul or whatever?'' Brittany questioned.

''Sure. I asked, I coaxed, I shouted. I tried reason, I tried the Bill of Rights, I tried everything I could think of. It didn't do much good. Although maybe that's what kept them from killing me outright, which is what they did with most of the prisoners they took.

''They threw me into this tiny cell and told me that my case was being reviewed. I kept telling them to call whatever representation our government had in the capital, and they kept saying it was being reviewed. They *reviewed* my case for two bloody years.

''I'd probably still be there if it hadn't been for this nun who came to visit the prisoners. I told her who I was. It turned out that she was the sister of the guy in charge of the jail. She believed me and convinced her brother to let me go. She probably threatened him with the wrath of God. For a nun, she was one feisty lady.

''That was a few weeks ago. I went to the American consul, and he got the paperwork moving.'' He shrugged. ''Here I am.''

''If you got out of prison a few weeks ago, what took you so long to get home?'' Brittany asked. ''Why didn't you call or write, let us know that you were alive?''

''I wasn't much to look at, honey. A year and a half in a Central American prison don't exactly leave you in prime physical condition. If I'd have come home then, I'd have scared everybody half to death.''

Michael tensed at the casual way he'd called Brittany ''honey'' and then forced himself to relax. Dan didn't know how much things had changed.

"Speaking of everyone—" Dan glanced at Michael, one brow raised in inquiry "—where's my mother? I went home tonight first, but the people who were living there seemed to think I might be a dangerous killer, and they wouldn't tell me anything. Did Mom sell the place?"

"About a year ago," Michael told him. He thrust his fingers through his hair, wishing there was some way to delay this conversation. His best friend had just come back from the dead, expecting to pick up the pieces of his life. How did he go about telling him that the pieces were so fragmented he was going to have to start over again?

"Where is she living now? An apartment? Somehow, I can't see Mom in an apartment."

Michael glanced at Brittany, but she hadn't taken her eyes off Dan since they'd sat down. Apparently, explanations were his department.

"Your mom is living in Europe. France, I think."

"Europe? Mom?" It was clear that didn't fit with the woman he remembered, and Michael knew his next piece of news wasn't going to make it easier.

"She's remarried."

Dead silence followed his words. Dan stared at him, his eyes startled. "Remarried? I don't believe it. When? To who?"

"About a year ago and to nobody that anybody knows. After your...the crash, she started traveling a lot. Maybe it hurt too much to stay here. Most people lost touch with her, and then we heard the house was on the market. Apparently she met someone in Europe and married him." Michael shrugged, wishing he had a more detailed explanation.

"Married." Dan shook his head slowly. "I can't believe it. I thought about a lot of things that might have changed while I was away, but I never thought of her remarrying. Do you have an address?''

''No. But I'd guess you could get it from the real estate agent. I know who sold the house.''

''Sure. I hadn't thought of that. I'll call them. I guess things have changed even more than I'd expected.''

*Was that ever an understatement.* Michael rubbed at the ache that was building in his forehead. How could he even begin to explain the changes that had taken place? There Dan sat, holding Brittany's hand. Michael wanted to pull her away from him and announce that she was his wife. But he couldn't do that. At least not quite so abruptly.

After what Dan had been through, how was he going to take the news that the woman he'd loved had married his best friend, that she'd had a child who now called that same best friend Daddy?

''Fill me in on the news.'' Dan's smile might have been forced, but it was clear that he didn't want to dwell on the melancholy. ''I feel as if I've been gone centuries instead of just a couple of years. The town has really grown. Is anybody we used to know still around?''

''A few,'' Michael said, feeling the ache intensify.

''I was surprised to see you here.'' Dan turned to Brittany, his eyes studying her as if he still couldn't believe she were there. ''This was the first place I thought of when I drew a blank at home. I figured I'd have to spend some time tracking you down.''

''I've...become rather close to the Sinclairs,'' Brittany murmured weakly, careful to avoid Michael's eyes.

"You couldn't get close to a greater bunch of people. This place was pretty much a second home to me."

Under other circumstances, Dan might have noticed the awkward silence that followed his remark. But he was still absorbing the fact that he was home at last.

"So, fill me in on what's been happening," he asked again. Michael drew a deep breath and began to talk, telling him what had happened to old friends—who'd married, who'd divorced, who had children. Dan listened, absorbing the small details like a man dying of thirst who'd finally been given water.

During his time in prison, there'd been little enough to fill his time, and he'd spent a lot of it thinking about the people back home, wondering what they were doing, trying to imagine what paths their lives might have taken. Foolish speculations but they'd helped to take his mind off his own situation.

Brittany listened to Michael's words with half an ear. She felt as if she had fallen into a dream and couldn't wake up. It just didn't seem possible that Dan was sitting next to her, holding her hand. How many times had she dreamed of just this, fantasized about it? In those first few months after the crash, she'd thought of little else.

But things had slowly changed. Her grief had been muted by time, her life filled with other things. Michael. Danielle. How were they going to explain things to him? He'd just come back from the dead. It seemed cruel to simply dump it all in his lap. And yet, her marriage to Michael, her child—Dan's child—those weren't the kind of things you could hide for long.

Brittany didn't know how long it had been since Michael had stopped speaking when the silence penetrated her absorption. Dan was staring at her, his thumb moving back and forth over her wedding ring. Her wedding ring. Her eyes met his, wondering if he'd realized the significance of the plain gold band. It was clear from his eyes that he had.

He looked more regretful than surprised, and Brittany felt a tremendous surge of guilt. He'd been through so much, lost so much. It didn't seem fair that he had to deal with yet more changes so soon after returning home.

"You're married," he said quietly, a statement, not a question.

Brittany opened her mouth, fumbling for an appropriate answer. She was vividly aware of Michael watching the awkward little exchange.

"It's not important," she blurted finally, thinking that this conversation could surely be postponed.

Dan's mouth twisted in a half smile, his eyes still sad. "I doubt if your husband would agree. Who is he? Anyone I know? Is he here tonight?"

Brittany stared at him, her mouth half-open as she sought the proper answers to his questions. He had a right to the truth, but she couldn't bring herself to hurt him.

Unconsciously, her eyes sought Michael's. More than two years of marriage had taught her that he could always be depended on. But for once, he couldn't help her. He seemed just as tongue-tied as she was. The silence stretched.

Dan looked from one to the other, suspicion flaring in the ice-blue depths of his eyes. His gaze dropped to Michael's left hand, which lay clenched against his knee.

"You bastard." The quiet words held a wealth of bitterness.

Michael felt the pain of betrayal as sharply as if it had been his and not Dan's. "It's not what you think," he said quietly.

"You and Brittany aren't married?"

"We're married."

"Then it's exactly what I think." He dropped Brittany's hand as if it had suddenly become contaminated, and he stood up.

Michael rose to his feet, his eyes meeting his friend's. "We need to talk about this," he began.

Hot rage flashed in Dan's eyes. Remembering the volatility of his temper, Michael braced himself, aware that Dan was just as likely to lash out with a fist as he was with words. But perhaps spending two years in a prison cell had taught him control.

"I don't think we have anything to say to each other."

"Dan, please. Listen to him." Brittany stood and set her hand on his arm, but he shook it off, the contempt in his eyes as searing as a hot brand.

"Save it. You're Michael's wife. That's all I want to know."

He spun on his heel and strode from the room without another word. Brittany took a step as if to follow him, but Michael caught her arm, stopping her.

"Let him go. He's not going to listen to either of us right now. Give him some time to cool off."

"He was so hurt," she whispered. The eyes she turned to him swam with tears. "Did you see the look in his eyes?"

"I saw it," he said grimly.

"I feel like we've just stabbed him in the back."

"We didn't." He released her arm. "Dan always

had a hot temper. He'll get over this and start thinking a little more rationally.''

"I hope so.''

Michael watched her, wondering if that was all she hoped. Did she hope that Dan would come back and open his arms and his heart to her again? It was clear that Dan had had no thought of anything else until he'd realized that she was married.

And she'd gone into his arms as if it were the only place in the world she wanted to be.

*Don't be a fool. Of course she was happy to see him. You felt the same. That doesn't mean she's still in love with him. You've had a lot of time with her. You've got a strong marriage. She's not going to walk out on that just because Dan has returned from the dead.*

*But she loved him. She had his child.*

*That was a long time ago. Danielle is your daughter in all the important ways. And Brittany is your wife.*

He wanted to let the little voice convince him, but doubt roiled in his gut. He kept hearing Dan ask about her marriage and Brittany saying that it wasn't important. Had she only been trying to avoid hurting Dan, or had she been speaking what was in her heart? Now that Dan was back, just how important was their marriage to her?

The answer to that question could have stilled the uneasiness, but he didn't ask. He was too afraid of the answer.

# Chapter Twelve

Christmas was a rather subdued holiday in the aftermath of Dan's appearance. This year, the Christmas feast was to be at Michael and Brittany's house, and Brittany had been looking forward to hosting the small family gathering.

But the joy had gone out of it. She kept looking at the snow outside, wondering where Dan was, wondering if he was warm enough, if he had enough to eat.

Michael entered the kitchen after she'd started the dinner preparations. His parents and Colin were due to arrive any minute. Danielle was perched on his hip, chewing on a cookie, more of the cookie getting on her face than into her mouth.

"How's everything going?"

"Fine."

They'd spoken very little since last night, each wrapped in thought. Last night, for the first time since they'd made their marriage a real one, they'd slept on opposite sides of the bed, carefully not touching.

"Is there anything I can do to help?" Michael asked politely.

"No thanks. I think everything is under control."

"So you wanted to put brown sugar on the turkey and vinegar on the ham?"

It took a moment for his words to penetrate. Brittany stared down at the box of brown sugar in her hand. She'd been carefully pressing the sweet substance to the turkey, while the ham sat looking forlorn under it's coating of vinegar. The two should have been mixed and used to coat the ham.

Muttering under her breath, she began dusting the sugar off the turkey. Luckily, it didn't seem inclined to stick to the snowy skin anyway. In a matter of minutes, the small turkey was in the oven, properly basted with butter this time. The ham received its coating and was set aside to wait its turn in the oven.

Brittany glanced over her shoulder at the window, frowning. Was the snow coming down harder than it had been?

"You keep looking out the window." Michael folded the top of the brown sugar box over with one hand, sealing it tight. "Are you looking for something?"

"No." But the guilty flush betrayed her.

"Thinking about Dan?" His tone was casual, but there was a hint of frost in his eyes. Unfortunately, Brittany wasn't looking at his eyes. She was once again looking out the window. It was definitely snowing harder now.

"I'm worried about him," she admitted.

"I told you, give him some time to cool off, and he'll be ready to listen to reason."

"I don't mean that," she said with a touch of impatience.

"What are you worried about, then?"

"I'm worried that he might not have a place to stay. Or enough money. Did you see his clothes? They were old and worn. What if he's out in this cold somewhere?"

Michael reined in his impatience, reaching for another cookie as Danielle polished off the one she had and held out a grubby hand for more. Right now, he didn't care if it did ruin her appetite. It was more important to keep her quiet and occupied.

After a sleepless night spent wondering if Brittany was regretting her marriage to him, the last thing he felt like doing was discussing Dan. There was nothing more to be said at this point. The look of worry in her eyes as she glanced at the window did nothing to soothe his ruffled feathers.

"I'm sure he's okay."

"How can you be sure? He just spent two years in some awful prison, and now he's come back to find that nothing is the way he left it. We shouldn't have let him go without making sure he was all right. We don't even know if he has any money."

"Brittany, one thing I know about Dan Remington and I'm willing to bet hasn't changed is that he's more than capable of taking care of himself. If he can survive a plane crash and prison, then I'm sure he can survive a winter day in Indiana."

He'd meant his words to be reassuring, but that wasn't how she took them.

"How can you be so callous." She slammed the refrigerator door shut, turning to look at him with a bunch of celery clenched in one fist as if it were a weapon. "He's supposed to be your best friend, but you don't seem to give a damn about him."

"I give more than a damn about him," Michael said tightly, his temper snapping. "But that doesn't mean I want him shoved down my damn throat along with the damn Christmas dinner. Dan is a survivor. He'll be fine. Do you think we could just forget about him for the rest of the day and try to enjoy the holiday?"

"I don't see how I can just forget about him, but I won't mention him again. I wouldn't want to spoil your damn dinner," she snapped.

"Damn." Danielle smiled at both of them as their eyes jerked to her angelic little face. "Damn." She seemed pleased with this new word and repeated it again with emphasis. "Damn."

"Now see what you've done." Brittany reached for the toddler as if to remove her from contaminating influences.

"Look what *I've* done? As I recall, I wasn't the only one slinging the word around."

Brittany flushed but refused to back down. "You're the one who started it."

"Actually, I think you were the first one to use the word in question."

"Damn." Danielle studied her cookie, clearly pleased with herself. Her parents stared at her, wondering how you explained to an almost two-year-old who was rapidly discovering the joys of language that some words weren't for repeating. Especially when they'd greeted every other word with lavish encouragement.

"Damn."

Their eyes met over her head. Michael was the first one to break. His mouth quivered and then widened in a smile that rapidly became a chuckle. Brittany looked as if she might hold on to her annoyance, but the obvious humor in the situation couldn't be denied. She laughed, hugging Danielle close. How was it that a child could always put something into perspective, even when she didn't know she was doing it?

"I guess we're going to have to watch our language from now on," Michael said, laughter still tinting his voice.

"I guess so."

He reached out to ruffle Danielle's silky, dark hair and was rewarded with a cookie-encrusted smile. "Let's hope she loses interest in it after a while."

"How are we going to explain this one to your parents?"

"Let's just keep her mouth full," Michael suggested.

"A coward's way out, but I like it."

The small quarrel broke the tension between them, but it didn't really solve anything.

During the past two years, they'd built a marriage based on friendship and mutual respect. It took something like this to show how shaky that foundation could be.

The days between Christmas and New Year's were tense. The one cardinal rule in their marriage had been that they didn't discuss their feelings for each other. It was enough that they were married and working toward the same goals. Not even in the darkness of their bedroom had either of them said anything about love.

It had worked well enough until now. Now, it was clear that they'd been existing as if they were acrobats working without a safety net. When something happened to shake the foundations of their marriage, they had nothing to fall back on.

Michael, uncertain of Brittany's feelings, withdrew emotionally and physically. He knew they should talk about Dan's return and what it might mean, if anything. But he was afraid to probe too deeply, afraid he might not like the answers he came up with.

Brittany didn't encourage a discussion. How could she discuss her feelings about Dan's return when she didn't know what they were?

Brittany leaned back in her chair, staring out the window at the snow that was drifting down. It had turned out to be an exceptionally cold winter, with more snow than usual. Despite Michael's assurances that Dan was a survivor, she couldn't help but wonder where he was, if he was all right.

It was almost three weeks into the new year, and as far as she knew, no one had heard from him since he walked out of Donovan and Beth's house on Christmas Eve. What if he never came back? There were so many unanswered questions, things she wanted to say to him, to ask him.

She picked up her pen, doodling on the edge of the grocery list she was supposed to be making. Danielle was sleeping in her room, and the house was quiet, that special kind of quiet that seemed to descend with the snow.

How *did* she feel about Dan?

It was a straightforward question. She should have been able to come up with a straightforward answer. She was happy that he was alive, that he was back. His death had been so senseless, such a waste of life. Seeing him alive and well was like seeing a miracle—

something you wanted so badly, even though you knew it could never happen.

She'd loved him once. In fact, she'd been sure that she'd love him always. She'd had his child. Wasn't that an indication of how deeply she'd cherished him and his memory?

Did she still love Dan? She knew the question was in Michael's eyes when he looked at her. It was a complicated question that couldn't simply be answered with a yes or no. She frowned, trying to define her feelings to herself. He'd been her first love. And he had, albeit unwittingly, given her Danielle. How could she not love someone who'd given her something so precious?

But it had been Michael who'd enabled her to have Danielle, to care for her. Michael who'd been there through mood swings and swollen ankles and childbirth. Michael who'd changed diapers, warmed bottles and walked the floor with a colicky infant. Dan might have been present at Danielle's conception, but he wasn't her father, not in the deepest sense of the word. That wasn't his fault, but it didn't change the facts.

But what about her own feelings? Her time with Dan seemed so long ago. She'd been a different person then. The Brittany who'd loved him didn't exist anymore.

And there was Michael. Always her thoughts circled around to him. They'd never said they loved each other. But that didn't mean that the emotions weren't there. *Did* Michael love her?

It was a relief when the doorbell rang. Anything was better than sitting here thinking and rethinking and getting nowhere. The snow had almost stopped. Maybe it was Beth.

But it wasn't Beth. Brittany's heart gave a bump when she saw who was standing outside the door.

"Dan."

"Hi. Maybe we should talk." He didn't smile and it was impossible to read anything in the ice blue of his eyes.

"Yes." She swallowed, summoning up a smile. "I think you're right. Come in."

He wiped his feet on the mat before stepping into the hall and shrugging out of his coat—not the thin jacket he'd been wearing Christmas Eve but a heavy sheepskin-lined one, more in keeping with the weather.

"I had a chance to do a little shopping." He must have noticed her looking at the coat.

"I'm glad. You didn't really look prepared for winter," she said, taking the coat and hanging it in the closet.

"I wasn't. I'd forgotten what bone-deep cold felt like."

"I suppose it was pretty warm...where you were." Brittany led the way into the living room, aware that she sounded very hostessy.

"Hot might be a better description," Dan said easily.

"I can imagine."

"No, I don't think you can." But there was no anger in the contradiction.

"You're probably right. I'm sorry. I didn't mean to sound like a handbook on how to make polite conversation."

"That's okay." He half smiled but it didn't reach his eyes. "The situation is a little awkward, I suppose."

"Yes."

Brittany sat on the sofa, and Dan chose a chair opposite her. Once seated, there was a momentary silence. She racked her brain for something to say. She'd once been in love with this man. Surely they couldn't be completely without words.

"I wanted to apologize for reacting the way I did the other night," Dan said, breaking the silence. "I had no right to act as if you'd committed some crime by marrying Michael."

"That's all right. I know it must have been a shock to you. So much has changed."

"That it has. You know I used to dream about you while I was in prison."

"Did you?" Brittany wasn't sure what she should feel at his admission. Flattered? Touched? Moved? She felt a little of all those emotions. But most of all, she felt a deep sadness for the time he'd lost. Time he could never regain.

"Yeah." He hunched his shoulders and looked around the living room, obviously sensing her discomfort. "So, what do you do these days?"

The change of subject was obvious, but Brittany was too grateful to mind.

"I stay home with—" She broke off, coughing. For a moment, she'd almost forgotten that he didn't know about Danielle. It seemed incredible that he had a daughter and didn't know it. "I...ah...stay home most of the time. I've been doing some writing. I've sold a couple of articles. Nothing major yet, but I keep working at it."

"That's great. I know you wanted to go into journalism. Did you switch majors?"

"I...ah...didn't get my degree, actually."

"You didn't?" He was surprised. "You only had another year to go. What happened?"

"It's rather a long story."

"I've got time. I'd like to know what's been happening in your life. It's obvious it didn't follow the scenarios I was building.''

His mouth twisted in a quirky smile that made her heart ache. He looked so alienated. What must it feel like to come back to find everything you'd known had changed almost beyond recognition?

She looked at him helplessly. He had a right to know about Danielle. After all, it hadn't been by his choice that he'd been denied knowledge of his child. She wasn't ready to tell him now, but then, maybe there was no such thing as being ready to tell a man he had a year-and-a-half-old daughter.

''Why don't I make a pot of coffee?'' She'd tell him but she needed a few minutes to gather her thoughts, put them in a coherent order.

''Sure. Coffee was something I missed while I was…away.''

''Well, I don't promise that it will be good. Michael usually makes the coffee around here…'' She trailed off, aware that the reminder that she shared this home with Michael had, perhaps, been illtimed. Dan said nothing, the half smile frozen in place. ''I'll go make the coffee,'' Brittany murmured.

In the kitchen, she reached for the filters and coffee automatically, her thoughts whirling. It seemed so strange to have Dan here. After the crash, memories of him had lingered in so many places—places they'd been to together. But this house had been associated with Michael only—there'd been nothing of Dan here. Now here he was, in one of the few places she'd never pictured him.

Her hand was shaky as she poured water into the coffee maker. She had to tell him about Danielle. He deserved to know, and she wanted him to hear it from her. The questions was *how* to tell him. Did she just blurt it out, or did she lead up to it carefully?

As it turned out, she didn't have to worry about how to tell him.

When she walked into the living room with the coffee, at first glance she thought he'd gone. A feeling of relief swept over her. If he'd gone, she'd been spared the ordeal of having to tell him anything. But then a movement caught the corner of her eye, and she turned to see Dan standing near the baby grand piano in the corner.

The piano had been a gift from Donovan and Beth on their first wedding anniversary. She dabbled on it a bit, but Michael was the one with the real talent. They'd spent a lot of wonderful evenings, especially in the winter, with Michael playing the piano and family and friends singing off-key and occasionally off-color songs.

"That's Michael's toy," she said casually, setting the cups down before approaching the piano. "He's quite good," she added with unconscious pride.

She had almost reached him when she noticed the rigidity of his back, the hand clenched into a fist at his side. It was only then that she realized what had caught his attention. It wasn't the piano he was looking at; instead, he'd been drawn to the photos that lined one corner of the grand. Photos of her and Michael and Danielle.

"Oh." The small exclamation escaped her as she lifted a hand to her throat.

"Yes, 'oh,'" he snarled. He spun away from the photos, and Brittany took a step backward when she saw the fury that glazed in his eyes.

"Dan, I was going to tell you. I didn't want you to find out this way."

"I just bet you didn't. Just how did you expect to tell me about this?"

"I thought we'd sit down over some coffee, and I could explain it to you."

"Explain it to me?" he asked incredulously. "Explain how you jumped into bed with my best friend the minute you heard I'd been killed?"

Brittany blinked at him, uncertain of his meaning. "That isn't how it was."

"No?" He turned and pointed at the photographs. "I'm no expert on babies, but that's not a newborn in those pictures. What did you do? Go straight from the funeral into his arms?

"My God, Brittany, I know it may have been a little naive of me to think you'd be waiting for me if and when I got home. But I sure as hell thought you'd grieve more than a day or two."

He spun away as if the sight of her made him physically ill. Brittany stared at his rigid back, trying to sort his words into some sensible pattern. Her eyes widened when she realized what was in his mind. He thought Danielle was Michael's child, that she had slept with Michael soon after he had been supposedly killed.

"No. Dan, it wasn't like that,"

"Don't give me that. What was it like, Brittany?" He turned toward her, his eyes narrowed. He looked as if he hated her. "Are you going to try and tell me that you were so overcome with grief, you didn't know what you were doing? Or did you just see Michael as a way out?"

"What are you talking about?"

"You were pushing me to get married before I left.

When I wouldn't bite and then was so inconsiderate as to turn up dead, did you turn to Michael? Play on his sympathies? Or did you just tumble into bed with him and then tell him you were pregnant? A strong sense of responsibility—that's Michael. He'd have married you in a minute."

The crack of her hand on his cheek was loud in the quiet house. His head jerked with the force of the blow which left a red welt across his face.

"You don't know what you're talking about."

"Then why don't you explain it to me." But the contempt in his eyes told her that he'd already made up his mind.

"I don't owe you an explanation," she said steadily. Their eyes locked in silent battle, neither giving an inch. A plaintive wail broke the tense standoff as Danielle announced that she was awake and not happy at being left alone.

Dan's jaw tightened. Brittany put up her chin. She was damned if she'd explain anything to him. How could she have forgotten that arrogant streak in him?

"I'd like you to leave now," she said quietly.

"With pleasure."

She didn't move as he turned and stalked to the door, snatching his coat out of the closet. He opened the door and then seemed to hesitate. He turned.

"You were all that kept me alive, you know." The anger seemed to have drained from him, leaving a soul-deep weariness that tore at her. "Thinking about you kept me sane. All those months, I kept fantasizing about what it would be like when I finally got home."

Danielle began to cry louder, unaccustomed to being ignored. Dan glanced in the direction of the sound.

"This sure as hell wasn't part of my fantasies."

He was gone before Brittany could say anything. The picture of him standing in the doorway, the snow drifting behind him, lingered in her mind a long time. He'd looked so alone.

Michael cursed as he bobbled a line, creating a new and rather exotic wall in the house he was supposed to be drafting. With a sigh, he threw down the pencil. It hadn't been going well, anyway. The preliminary stages of a design were usually fun because almost anything was still possible. This project wasn't working out that way.

But then, nothing had been much fun lately. Not since Christmas. Dan's return had been like a live stick of dynamite landing in the middle of his life. He hadn't realized just how fragile the foundations of his marriage were until now.

If asked, he would have said that he and Brittany had a strong relationship. They didn't need mushy declarations of affection. But now he was beginning to think that a few mushy declarations might make him feel a whole lot better.

Just how did Brittany feel about him? Affection? Passion? She cared about him. He'd have to be blind not to see that. But did it go deeper than that? Their sex life was good, more than good—it was downright terrific.

But there had to be more to it than that. Affection. Sex. Those things weren't enough to build a marriage on. He ran his hand through his hair, staring at the drafting board without seeing it. A marriage took... love.

And that was exactly what he felt for Brittany—what he'd felt for a long time. It was hard to remember a time when he hadn't loved her. Even when he'd first met her, he'd been drawn to her. But she'd been his best friend's girl, and he'd buried that awareness so deep he hadn't even been able to admit to himself why he was marrying her, why he'd wanted to stay married to her.

And during the past couple of years, he hadn't had to contemplate his feelings. After all, he'd had Brittany and Danielle. Why would he need to analyze what he felt about them?

It was only when something happened that threatened the even keel of his life that he took the time to really look at what she meant to him, at what it would mean to lose her.

A knock on the door broke into his thoughts and he turned, running a hand over his hair, trying to put on a professional face.

"Come in."

He felt the professional face stiffen into a mask when Dan walked into the room, closing the door behind him.

"Dan. What a...surprise." The words held a flat note, but he was helpless to project more enthusiasm into them. This man had been his best friend, almost a brother, yet now he was first and foremost a potential rival. And Michael was discovering a possessive streak he hadn't known he had.

"Michael." Dan stood just inside the door, his hands in the pockets of his jeans, his eyes skimming over the room without really seeing it. "Great office."

"Thanks. It's adequate."

"I've run into some of our old friends, and they tell me you're doing well." The words did not sound very complimentary.

"I do all right," Michael admitted cautiously. He could feel the tension in the other man. There was some purpose behind this visit.

"Looks like you're doing better than all right." Dan smiled thinly, his eyes cool. "Great job, great house, great wife. Great kid."

There was a beat pause before he added the last, and Michael tensed. So Dan knew about Danielle.

"You've been to see Brittany."

"Yeah, I've been to see Brittany. You lousy son of a bitch!"

The punch came too quickly for Michael to do more than duck back so that it caught him on the edge of the chin instead of breaking his jaw as it might have if it had connected as intended.

He blocked the next one, catching Dan's wrist, using the hold to spin the other man around and slam him face first into the wall.

"What the hell was that for?" he panted, pinning Dan against the wall with his superior weight.

"You know what it's for." Dan heaved backward but he couldn't dislodge Michael. Two years in prison had taken their toll.

The door crashed open and Donovan strode into the room, taking in the situation at a glance.

"Let him up, Michael."

"Why? So he can try and tear my head off again?" But he stepped back, eyeing Dan cautiously as he felt the tender spot on his chin. Dan spun, his eyes burning hatred as he leaned against the wall, out of breath.

"What's the problem here?"

"I don't know. He came into my office and took a swing at me."

"Dan?"

Dan shrugged his jacket back into place, throwing Donovan a quick glance. "This is something between Michael and I. Nobody else."

"When you start a fight in the offices of my company, that makes it my business." Donovan paused, looking from one to the other. "If this is about what I think it's about, I'd suggest that the two of you sit down and talk before you start throwing punches again." He turned to leave but stopped in the doorway. "You might try remembering that you were friends once."

The door shut behind him, and each man was silent, trying to anticipate the other's next move. Dan smoothed a hand over his hair.

"He's right, you know," Michael said, leaning back against the desk. "We need to talk. We should have done it before this."

"I don't know what there is to talk about." Dan seemed more weary than angry.

"Brittany, for one. And Danielle."

"Danielle? You named your kid after me? My God, Michael, that's rich." He laughed bitterly. "You actually named her after me. God, don't you have any shame at all?"

"Shame?" Michael's brows rose. "What have I got to be ashamed about?"

Dan stared at him as if he couldn't believe the question. "You don't think there's something wrong with having married the woman *I* loved?"

"We thought you were dead. Besides, it didn't seem like there was much choice at the time."

"Not much choice? You mean I was right? She actually got pregnant and that's why you married her?"

"I thought you said you talked to Brittany." Michael

frowned, feeling as if he were missing some vital piece of the conversation.

"I did talk to her."

"What did she tell you?"

Dan shrugged. "She said you make the coffee. She's working on her writing. And you play piano."

"What did she say about our marriage? The baby?"

"She didn't have to say anything," Dan told him, anger flaring in his eyes again. "I saw the pictures. You and her and the baby. My God, did you even wait till I was cold in my supposed grave?"

Michael leaned back, enlightenment dawning. "You saw the pictures and jumped to a bunch of conclusions, and you either walked out without talking to Brittany or you said awful things to her and she threw you out."

"More the latter than the former." Dan reached up to touch his cheek.

"You jackass. You haven't changed a bit. You're still always going off half-cocked without waiting for an explanation."

"The cozy little family portraits didn't seem to need much explanation," Dan snapped, annoyed with Michael's half-amused tone.

"Things aren't always what they seem, if you don't mind me being a little trite."

"As a matter of fact, I *do* mind. If there's some *explanation* for the fact that you jumped right into bed with Brittany as soon as I was out of the way, then I'd like to hear it."

"I don't know why I should bother to tell you, but I will because I think you have a right to know." Michael stood up, moving to the window to stare out at the snowy landscape. His voice was quiet when he began speaking.

"I did marry Brittany because she was pregnant. We got married a couple of months after the crash."

"A couple of months? That's all the time you waited?"

"That's all we waited." Michael turned from the window, his eyes on Dan. "Brittany was carrying your child."

He saw the impact of the words. Dan actually took a step back, his eyes disbelieving.

"My child?" he choked out. "She was pregnant when I left?" He read the answer in Michael's eyes and turned away, running a shaking hand through his hair. "My God, I had no idea. She didn't tell me. Why didn't she tell me? I'd never have left her alone if I'd known."

"She didn't want you to marry her because she was pregnant. She wanted to be sure you loved her."

"'Loved her'? I adored her. We quarreled before I left," he said slowly, remembering. "I hated that. I tried to call her from L.A., but I got hold of her parents, and they told me she was out. I was going to call her again when we got to the site, as soon as I could find a phone. Only we never reached the site."

He sank into a chair, his expression dazed. "A baby. I have a child."

Michael turned away, feeling a stab of pain in his chest. It hurt to hear Dan refer to Danielle as *his* child. He wanted to protest that she'd belonged to him since the moment the doctor put her in his hands. But he said nothing.

It took Dan a few minutes to absorb the shock. "I can't believe it. I have a daughter and I don't even know how old she is."

"She'll be two in March."

"Two. Two years old." Dan rubbed his hands over his face, grief flashing through his eyes.

Michael felt a twinge of pity. He'd been there for the first two years of Danielle's life. He knew just how terrible Dan's loss was.

"I...how did you end up marrying Brittany?" Dan asked at last, still struggling to comprehend the way his whole life seemed to have been turned upside down in a matter of minutes.

"She was alone." Michael shrugged. "She needed help."

"What about her parents?"

"They felt that she'd shamed them by getting pregnant. They wanted her to go off and have the baby and then give it up. She left. When I found her, she was living in a shabby apartment in a neighborhood I wouldn't send my worst enemy to. She had no insurance. She was running out of money. I talked her into marrying me, at least until the baby was born."

"Why?" Dan stared at him, trying to imagine what had happened.

Michael shrugged again. "I told myself I was doing it for you."

"For me?"

"You were my best friend. Brittany was carrying your child. I thought you were dead, and it seemed like the only thing left that I could do for you was to make sure Brittany and your baby were all right."

"You said you 'told' yourself you were doing it for me?"

Michael hesitated and then looked up, his eyes meeting Dan's. "I don't think that was the whole reason."

"I don't think so, either. I mean, we were friends, but that's going a little bit above and beyond the call of duty.'' There was no rancor in Dan's voice. ''I suppose I should thank you for taking care of them.''

''That's not necessary.''

''You love her, don't you?''

''I love her.''

The flat statement hung in the air between them. Michael had staked a claim, making it clear that whatever had happened in the past, he now regarded Brittany as his. Friendship, past or present, didn't have the strength of his ties to her. He wasn't going to give her up easily.

If Dan wanted her, he was going to have to fight for her.

# Chapter Thirteen

Dinner that night was a silent affair. Michael was waiting for Brittany to tell him about Dan's visit. Brittany was still wrestling with the realization that she hadn't been as hurt as she should have been by Dan's harshness.

There was a time when having Dan think badly of her would have broken her heart. Now, it was upsetting but hardly the end of the world. She didn't love him anymore. And that hurt more than the cruel accusations he'd made. In the beginning she'd been so sure that she'd love him forever, that if only he'd return, her life would be complete.

But he hadn't returned, and her life had been pretty fulfilling without him. She looked across the table at Michael, who was eating his dinner with a dogged determination that made it clear he had only the vaguest idea of what was on his plate.

Michael had completed her life. Brittany stared at him, feeling a shock of awareness. Without Michael, her life would be so empty.

He looked up, catching her eyes on him. He arched one brow in inquiry, but Brittany shook her head and looked down at her plate. What a time to suddenly realize that you were in love with your husband. There should have been candlelight and flowers and soft music.

How long had she loved him? It seemed like forever. The feeling had been inside of her for so long. How could she not have known it? He was good and kind but never boring. He made her laugh, he believed in her, encouraged her to be happy. As a lover, he was wildly exciting, teaching her things about herself she'd never known.

"I think it's about time Danielle went to bed. She's about to fall asleep in her peas."

Brittany's head snapped up, her thoughts so far removed from toddlers and strained peas that it took her a second to register what he was saying.

"Oh. Right." She pushed back her chair, reaching for the tray on Danielle's high chair. "It is pretty late for her to be up." She lifted the baby out of the chair, soothing her when she began to fuss irritably.

Michael watched Brittany leave the room before pushing back his own chair and reaching for their plates. From the looks of Brittany's dinner, she hadn't had much appetite. He carried the plates into the kitchen and began stacking them in the dishwasher, his movements made jerky by irritation.

Didn't she plan to tell him about Dan's visit at all? Did she think he wouldn't find out? And why would she want to hide it from him? From what Dan had said, it hadn't been a terribly pleasant encounter. Unless it had hurt her so badly she couldn't talk about it. And for it to hurt that much, she'd have to care about Dan very deeply.

He slammed a glass into the dishwasher with enough force to break it. Muttering under his breath, he fished the broken chunks out of the silverware tray and dropped them into the trash.

"What happened?"

He turned quickly at the sound of Brittany's voice. Seeing her, he wanted to take her in his arms, tell her he loved her, tell her he'd never let her go.

"Michael?" Her tone made it clear that she found his behaviour odd, and he shook his head, turning back to flip on the dishwasher.

"I broke a glass."

"You didn't cut yourself, did you?"

"No." *God, you're pretty far gone when you find yourself wishing you had cut yourself just so she could fuss over it.*

He leaned against the counter, looking at her. "Dan came to see me today."

Brittany's head jerked up, her eyes startled. "He did?"

"He said he'd already seen you."

"Yes, he did. I was going to tell you, but it wasn't a very pleasant visit." She pushed her hands into the pockets of her jeans, looking away from him. "He found out about Danielle, more or less."

"So I gathered. He seemed to have the wrong impression, though."

Her eyes flickered to his and then away. "Did you tell him the truth?"

"That he was Danielle's father? I told him."

"Everything?"

"Everything. Why we married, the whole thing."

"How did he react?"

"Just about the way you'd expect. He was stunned, a little hurt, maybe."

She sighed, pulling one hand out of her pocket to run it through her hair. "We made such a mistake," she said, thinking that they should have told Dan the whole truth that first night.

What Michael heard was that their marriage had been a mistake.

"No." He moved so quickly that Brittany didn't have a chance to react. She gasped as he caught her upper arms, pulling her against his body. Startled, she looked up into eyes that blazed a fiery blue. "Don't ever say that."

"Say wh—" His mouth smothered her confused question, his arms sweeping around her to crush her so close she could hardly draw a breath.

He didn't ask for her surrender. He demanded it. His tongue plunged into her mouth, sweeping across the tender surfaces as if to conquer them, make them his own.

Brittany's hands pressed against his chest in automatic protest before slowly relaxing and sliding upward to circle his neck. Her fingers burrowed into the silky, dark hair at the nape of his neck as her mouth opened to him, her tongue coming up to fence with his.

He dragged his mouth from hers, but only to find the warm skin of her neck. Brittany's head fell back, her fingers clinging to his shoulders as his tongue found the pulse that pounded raggedly at the base of her throat.

Her head spun with the quick rise of passion. He wasn't giving her time to think, and there was something she needed to think about. But the knowledge was a foggy, far-off thing, without urgency.

He pushed her away just long enough to strip the sweatshirt over her head, and then his hands were cupping her breasts, the nipples growing taut beneath his fingers. She was vaguely aware that he was shifting her backward, but it didn't really register until his hands closed over her waist and he lifted her onto the dining room table.

"Michael!" She'd meant it to be a protest, but it came out as more of a whimper as his mouth closed over one swollen nipple, teasing it with lips and tongue until it throbbed. Satisfied, he switched his attentions to the other breast, drawing a sob of pleasure from her throat.

Not until he'd reduced her to quivering awareness did he lift his head, catching her mouth in a long, drugging kiss.

"Tell me you want me," he whispered against her lips.

"I want you." How could he think she didn't? Couldn't he feel how she burned for him?

He unsnapped her jeans, lifting her as he slid them and her panties off her legs, tossing them both aside. The table was cool against her bare skin, a vivid contrast to the heat of him. When had he taken off his clothes? she wondered distractedly.

His hand slid up her thigh as he eased her back on the table, and she trembled when his fingers found her. He stroked the moist flesh of her, drawing a ragged whimper of pleasure as he slipped a finger inside, feeling the heat of her.

"Tell me again," he said against her breast.

"I want you," she gasped. His tongue swirled lazily

across her belly. "I want you." His hand probed deeper, taking possession of her. "I want you. Ah, Michael."

She arched, her hands clenching in his hair as his mouth found her, his tongue tasting her passion. Brittany kept her eyes closed, sparks of red fire darting across her vision as her body responded helplessly to his ministrations.

He drove her relentlessly, rushing her toward the peak so that when it came, she fell breathlessly into it, hardly aware of herself anymore.

The last pulsating sensation had not yet died when she felt him over her. She opened dazed eyes as he wrapped his hands in her hair, holding her still as he looked down at her, watching every flicker of expression as he slowly filled her with his strength.

"Michael." Something flared in his eyes when she spoke his name. Where before, he'd rushed her toward a climax, now he seemed intent on taking his time. Now it was Brittany who quivered with impatience, her hands on his hips urging him to pick up the pace. He smiled, his eyes still holding that watchful look, and slowed until he was barely moving, seeming to take pleasure in the fact that she so blatantly wanted more than he was giving.

"What's the hurry, sweetheart?"

"Please." The breathless little moan was all she could manage, her head tossing back and forth, scattering thick black hair across the pale wood.

His laughter held pure masculine triumph, but he gave her what she wanted. Brittany's hands sought purchase on his damp back, needing something to cling to as the world exploded into a million sparkling pieces all around her.

His voice came to her through a fog, low and husky, holding a note of promise. "We've got all night, and this is only the beginning."

It was a promise he kept, and it was a night neither of them was likely to forget. Brittany lost count of the number of times he made love to her. He carried her into the bedroom, laying her across the bed and bringing her to sweet ecstasy again and again until she begged for mercy. And then he carried her into the shower, supporting her trembling body with his as the warm water sluiced over them and he proved to her that she wasn't as tired as she thought.

When she finally fell asleep, it was almost dawn. She slept deeply, dreamlessly, not waking until Danielle's plaintive cry dragged her from the arms of Morpheus. She staggered out of bed, fumbling for a robe as she went down the hall to the baby's room. She changed Danielle, lifting her onto her hip to carry her into the living room, then setting her on the floor.

Michael was gone. That much was clear. She wasn't sure if she was glad or sorry. Still rubbing sleep from her eyes, she began to warm a bottle for Danielle and make a pot of coffee for herself.

Every muscle in her body ached, every nerve ending tingled from the night before. She felt achingly tired and startlingly alive at the same time. Still, there was something odd about the whole thing. It was as if he'd been trying to prove something to her.

Brittany poured a cup of coffee and sipped it, feeling the caffeine enter her system, banishing some of the fog from her brain. What had set him off? She frowned at the coffee maker. It wasn't as though she'd been wearing anything particularly sexy or had said anything provocative. In fact, they'd been talking about Dan right before Michael had jumped her bones.

She'd just said something about them having made a mistake. And he'd said no. No what? No, it wasn't a mistake. But what wasn't a mistake? She'd meant that they should have told Dan the truth right away. Was it possible that Michael thought she'd meant something else altogether? Their marriage?

"He couldn't think that," she muttered out loud, reaching for the bottle and testing it against her wrist.

But if he *had* thought that... Would that explain last night? Maybe he'd been trying to prove something to her, to make her see that they were compatible? She flushed, remembering the abandoned response she'd given him. Well, there was no doubt he'd proved that.

She carried the bottle into Danielle, who took it eagerly. Brittany was halfway to the bedroom to get some clothes on when the doorbell rang. Glancing at the clock and then at the rather scruffy terry robe she'd thrown on, she went to answer it. If it was a salesman, he was going to get short shrift from her.

She pulled open the door, the words of polite dismissal dying on her lips. "Dan."

"Hi." There was a short silence while they stared at each other. "I've come to apologize," Dan said at last, his uneasiness obvious.

"Come in."

"Thanks. I wouldn't blame you if you booted me out."

Brittany shut the door, reaching up to push her hair back from her face, wishing she'd had a chance to comb it or brush her teeth or get properly dressed. After last night, she could have used a little time to pull herself together before having to deal with apologies from anyone.

"You've been under a lot of strain." She shrugged. "I don't blame you for jumping to conclusions."

"It was stupid of me," he said as he pulled off his coat and draped it over a chair.

"A little." She smiled, taking the sting out of the words. "I've made some coffee. Would you like some?"

Dan's eyes went past her, his face suddenly whitening. Brittany turned, comprehension dawning when she saw Danielle toddling toward her, bottle clutched in one hand.

"Hi, sweetie. Did you come to see who Mama was talking to?" She bent to scoop the little girl up, turning with her in her arms. "Danielle, this is Dan. He's a…friend."

Dan stared at the child, his face pale. Danielle looked at him for a minute and then turned away, more interested in the collar of her mother's bathrobe than she was in this stranger.

"She's beautiful," Dan said softly. Brittany glanced at him and then looked away. There was too much vulnerability in his eyes. No one should see another person that naked.

"Thank you."

"May I hold her?" There was so much hunger in the question, so much pain that Brittany felt her eyes sting.

"Of course. Why don't you take her into the living room while I change and get us some coffee?"

She pretended not to notice that his hands were not quite steady as he took Danielle from her. Danielle stared at him, trying to decide whether or not she approved of this person holding her. He appeared to pass some test, because she stuck her bottle in her mouth, watching him over it with wide blue eyes.

Satisfied that they were going to be all right, Brittany made a quick trip to the bathroom, splashing water on her face and running a comb through her hair before tugging on a pair of jeans and a sweater. There was a faint bruise on her shoulder, and she flushed, remembering Michael's hands on her. She'd be willing to bet that his back bore the marks of her nails.

Shaking her head, she forced her mind back to the present. Last night required some thinking, and she couldn't do it with Dan waiting in the living room.

When she came back out, he was sitting on the floor with Danielle, carefully stacking blocks so that she could knock them over with one blow. It was one of her favorite games. Brittany brought cups of coffee into the living room, sitting one on a table near Dan, holding the other close to her chest.

He looked up at her as she sat on the sofa, drawing one leg under her.

"She's truly beautiful. You and Michael have done a wonderful job." The compliment was given freely, and Brittany accepted it in the manner given.

"Thank you. We think she's a pretty terrific kid ourselves."

It was funny how she could look at him and feel nothing more than a nostalgic fondness. There was no more doubt, no more wondering what might have been. He was silent for a long moment, watching the child.

"I'd never have left if I'd known you were pregnant," he said at last.

"I know. I always knew that."

"If I'd known— We would have married. I wonder

if we'd have been happy?'' He seemed to be speaking more to himself than to her, trying to look at a path not taken.

''I don't know. I used to think about it a lot. Wonder what it would have been like.''

''You don't think about it much anymore, do you?'' He glanced up, his eyes catching hers. Brittany wasn't sure what answer he hoped for, but she couldn't give him anything but the truth.

''Not much,'' she said gently.

He nodded, looking back at Danielle, who was stacking blocks into an extremely shaky tower.

''She has my eyes.'' The comment might have been random, but Brittany thought she understood. He'd come back to find that everything he'd left behind was gone, never to be regained. He needed some connection, however small, to the life he might have had, the person he'd once been.

''She has your eyes,'' Brittany agreed.

The answer seemed to satisfy him. He reached out to steady the blocks.

''I suppose I really came to say goodbye,'' he said at last, without looking at her.

''You're leaving?'' She was surprised. ''You just got home.''

''There's really not much here for me. I got my mother's address from the agent who sold the house. I thought I'd take a trip to Europe, see how she's doing. We spoke on the phone and she was going to fly home, but I told her I'd rather come to her. After two years in the tropics, the winter doesn't suit my bones.'' He gave an exaggerated shiver, his mouth twisting in a half smile.

Brittany didn't think his leaving had anything to do

with the weather, but she didn't argue. Maybe he was right. There didn't seem to be much left for him here.

"We'll miss you, Michael and I. We're just now getting used to knowing you're alive."

"I don't think Michael will miss me all that much," Dan said ruefully. "I think he'll be relieved to see me gone. Not that he isn't glad I'm all right," he added. "But there's a real possessive streak in him. One I never suspected."

Brittany flushed, well aware that he was referring to her. The idea that Michael was possessive of her was not displeasing.

Dan hadn't taken his eyes off Danielle, as if he were trying to store up memories of her for when he was gone.

"You'll always be welcome here, Dan. When she's old enough to understand, we plan to tell her about you. I know she'll want to know you."

He was quiet so long, she wondered if he'd even heard her, but his hand was clenched over a block, the knuckles turning white.

"Thanks," he said finally, his voice husky. "I'd like a chance to know her."

He stood up not long after that, announcing that he ought to be on his way. Brittany didn't try to persuade him to stay. She was not entirely at ease around him. There was a lingering feeling that she should feel something more for him, some deeper tie than she did.

They stood in the hallway for a moment without speaking. He reached out to take her hands, and Brittany didn't protest. His touch aroused nothing in her but a warm feeling for someone she cared about. His eyes searched hers, a rueful smile twisting his mouth at what he saw there.

"I'll always think that we could have had something good together. But I'm glad you're happy. Truly glad. And I'm glad you're happy with Michael. He's a hell of a guy."

"I know you'll find someone, Dan. And whoever she is, she'll be a lucky woman."

"Thanks. I may come to you for a reference."

His smile faded as his hands tightened over hers, and he bent to kiss her. It was a light kiss, a farewell, a fleeting gesture to what might have been, and Brittany accepted it as such.

A wave of cold air swept into the hallway, and Dan stepped back from Brittany, turning to look at Michael, who'd stopped dead in the doorway. A muscle ticked in Michael's jaw when he saw their linked hands. It was obvious that he'd seen the last of the kiss and, despite the perfect innocence of the situation, Brittany felt a twinge of uneasiness at the look in his eyes.

"You always did have a rotten sense of timing, Michael," Dan said calmly, dropping Brittany's hands and reaching for his coat.

"Should I remember to knock before entering my own home?" Michael's eyes followed Dan's every movement as if looking for an excuse to pounce.

"Don't be an idiot, Michael." Brittany stepped forward, setting her hand on his arm, feeling the tautness of the muscles beneath her fingers. "Dan is leaving."

"Good," he said bluntly.

Her fingers tightened chidingly. "I mean he's leaving Remembrance."

"Why?" Michael addressed the question to Dan. The other man shrugged into his coat before answering.

"There's really not much for me here."

Brittany felt the arm beneath her fingers relax as his meaning sank in.

"Where are you going?"

"I thought I'd head for Europe. I guess I've got a stepfather now. I probably ought to meet him."

"I hope you have a safe trip," Michael said quietly.

"Thanks."

Michael held out his hand. Dan looked at it for a moment before taking it. The handclasp was tight, their eyes meeting over it, saying things neither of them could say out loud. They'd been friends most of their lives, closer than most brothers. Saying goodbye wasn't easy.

"Well." Dan cleared his throat as his hand left Michael's. "I guess I'd better be on my way." He looked from Brittany to Michael. "Take care of that little girl in there. She's special."

"We will," Brittany told him, slipping her hand through Michael's arm. "You take care of yourself."

"Hell, I've come back from the dead once. I don't intend to tempt fate again." He lifted his hand and then was gone, the door shutting behind him.

Brittany reached up to wipe a tear from her cheek, her eyes bright. Looking down at her, Michael swallowed hard.

"If you want to go with him, I won't stop you," he said huskily, the words dragged from him.

Her eyes met his and she felt her heart swell at what she read there. "Why would I want to go with him when I have everything I want right here?"

"I just thought—" He broke off, his eyes dropping to where her hand rested on his arm. "You loved him."

"Yes, I did. But I loved him the way a girl loves. I

love you the way a woman loves. And it's so much stronger."

She saw the impact of her words in the way his eyes jerked to hers, the color seeping up in his face and then receding, leaving him pale.

"You love me?"

"More than anything in the whole world," she said, her voice shaky.

"Oh God." His arms swept around her, crushing her to him, and she gasped. "I love you so much. I didn't even realize how much until Dan came back and I thought I might lose you."

"Never. You'll never lose me," she promised. His kiss smothered anything she might have added, but there was really no need to say more. The kiss said it all.

A cranky wail from the living room brought them slowly apart. Brittany stared up at him with eyes shining with love, seeing the same emotion reflected back at her.

"I love you."

"I love you, Brittany. I don't know what I'd do without you."

"You won't have to find out," she assured him.

The wail grew in volume, demanding attention. She linked her arm with his, leaning her head on his shoulder. "I think Danielle is having trouble with some of the finer points of constructing a high rise. Maybe her Daddy could give her some pointers."

**A showgirl, a minister—
and an unsolved murder.**

# EASY VIRTUE

Eight years ago Mary Margaret's father was
convicted of a violent murder she knew he
didn't commit—and she vowed to clear his
name. With her father serving a life sentence,
Mary Margaret is working as a showgirl in Reno
when Reverend Dane Barrett shows up with
information about her father's case. Working to
expose the real killer, the unlikely pair also
proceed to expose themselves to an unknown
enemy who is intent on keeping the past buried.

**From the bestselling author of
LAST NIGHT IN RIO**

Available in December 1997
at your favorite retail outlet.

**The Brightest Stars in Women's Fiction.™**

# *Daniel MacGregor is at it again...*

### *New York Times* bestselling author

# NORA ROBERTS

introduces us to a new generation of MacGregors
as the lovable patriarch of the illustrious MacGregor
clan plays matchmaker again, this time to his three
gorgeous granddaughters in

## THE MACGREGOR BRIDES

Don't miss this brand-new continuation of Nora Roberts's
enormously popular *MacGregors* miniseries.

Available in November 1997
at your favorite retail outlet.

Don't miss this chance to get these popular titles
from *New York Times* bestselling author

# BARBARA DELINSKY

| | | | |
|---|---|---|---|
| #83250 | CHANCES ARE | $4.50 U.S. ☐ | |
| #83251 | SECRET OF THE STONE | $4.50 U.S. ☐ | |
| #83262 | THREATS AND PROMISES | $4.50 U.S. ☐ | |
| #83264 | FIRST, BEST AND ONLY | $4.50 U.S. ☐ | |
| #83290 | TWELVE ACROSS | $4.50 U.S. ☐ | |
| #83293 | A SINGLE ROSE | $4.50 U.S. ☐ | $4.99 CAN. ☐ |
| #66010 | T.L.C. | $4.99 U.S. ☐ | $5.50 CAN. ☐ |
| #66026 | FULFILLMENT | $4.99 U.S. ☐ | $5.50 CAN. ☐ |
| #66039 | THROUGH MY EYES | $4.99 U.S. ☐ | $5.50 CAN. ☐ |
| #66068 | CARDINAL RULES | $4.99 U.S. ☐ | $5.50 CAN. ☐ |
| #66077 | MONTANA MAN | $4.99 U.S. ☐ | $5.50 CAN. ☐ |
| #66061 | THE DREAM | $5.50 U.S. ☐ | $5.99 CAN. ☐ |
| #66161 | THE DREAM UNFOLDS | $5.50 U.S. ☐ | $6.50 CAN. ☐ |
| #66175 | THE DREAM COMES TRUE | $5.50 U.S. ☐ | $6.50 CAN. ☐ |
| #66271 | HAVING FAITH | $5.50 U.S. ☐ | $6.50 CAN. ☐ |
| #66287 | THE OUTSIDER | $5.50 U.S. ☐ | $6.50 CAN. ☐ |

**(limited quantities available on certain titles)**

|  |  |
|---|---|
| **TOTAL AMOUNT** | $ |
| **POSTAGE & HANDLING** | $ |
| ($1.00 for one book, 50¢ for each additional) | |
| **APPLICABLE TAXES\*** | $ _____ |
| **TOTAL PAYABLE** | $ _____ |
| (check or money order—please do not send cash) | |

To order, complete this form and send it, along with a check or money order for **the** total above, payable to MIRA Books, to: **In the U.S.:** 3010 Walden Avenue, P.O. Box 9077, Buffalo, NY 14269-9077; **In Canada:** P.O. Box 636, Fort Erie, Ontario, L2A 5X3.

Name: _____

Address: _____ City: _____

State/Prov.: _____ Zip/Postal Code: _____

\*New York residents remit applicable sales taxes.
Canadian residents remit applicable GST and provincial taxes.

MIRA BOOKS

Look us up on-line at: http://www.romance.net

MBDBL11

# Indiscreet

Camilla Ferrand wants everyone, especially her dying grandfather, to stop worrying about her. So she tells them that she is engaged to be married. But with no future husband in sight, it's going to be difficult to keep up the pretense. Then she meets the very handsome and mysterious Benedict Ellsworth who generously offers to accompany Camilla to her family's estate—as her most devoted fiancé.

But at what cost does this *generosity* come?

**From the bestselling author of** *Impulse*

# CANDACE CAMP

Available in November 1997
at your favorite retail outlet.

*\*Candace Camp also writes for Silhouette® as Kristen James*

**MIRA** **The brightest star in women's fiction**

Look us up on-line at: http://www.romance.net

MCCIND

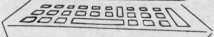